BEST
BISEXUAL
WOMEN'S
EROTICA

BEST BISEXUAL WOMEN'S EROTICA

Edited by

Cara Bruce

CLEIS
PRESS

Published in the United States by Cleis Press Inc.,
P.O. Box 14697, San Francisco, California 94114.

Printed in the United States.
Cover design: Scott Idleman
Cover photograph: Regine Mahaux/Getty Images
Text design: Karen Quigg
Logo art: Juana Alicia

This book is dedicated to all my lovers, men and women, past and present. Thank you to everyone who has helped me with their guidance and support: Marcy Sheiner, Thomas Roche, Rachel Kramer Bussel, Lisa Montanarelli, Violet Blue, Annalee Newitz, Carol Queen, Susie Bright, Felice Newman, and, of course, my mom.

TABLE OF CONTENTS

Introduction
Cara Bruce

Most people seem to think bisexual women have a magical ability to have their cake and eat it, too. This perception makes them sometimes the most hated and other times the most lusted after sexual group under the rainbow. In a way, bi women have become the ultimate pornographic symbol. Nowadays, it's rare to find a mainstream porn film without your token "girl-on-girl" scene (I think they actually call those films lacking girl-girl action "gay male"). Why is this?

For straight men, seeing two or more women in steamy scenarios seems to offer a glimpse into the compelling and arousing mysteries of women. For women, it offers an image of themselves as supersexual: The bisexual woman is the one who will try anything, who is comfortable enough with her sexuality to act on her same-gender desires. Women who don't know much about lesbianism, or are curious about experimenting, view bisexual women—the cake eaters—as women they can not only relate to, but also learn from. Certainly I, like many of my bi friends, have taught a "straight" woman a thing or two. And while gay and bisexual men are not yet really accepted by the "mainstream," two women together seem, to many, "safe."

Bisexual women are a staple of everyone else's porn and erotica, and maybe that's why you rarely see collections specifically *by* and *for* them. In that sense, this collection is the first chance for bisexual women to explicitly reveal themselves, their sex lives, and their desires. I was ecstatic when Cleis Press asked me to edit this collection. To me, this project reflected the joys, difficulties, and exquisite range of sexual encounters that come with being a bisexual woman.

One thing I discovered was that a lot of people's misconceptions about bisexual behavior showed up in many of the stories I received as submissions. A large percentage of stories featured predictably scripted threeways, a pointedly straight woman experimenting for the first time, or a lesbian stepping out with a man. Sure, every group is stereotyped in some way, but I have to admit I was surprised to see that in our information-addled era, the urban-legends-as-sexual-fantasies still loomed so large.

So where do all of these misconceptions about bisexual women come from? While the fantasy bisexual woman appears as a sex-loving goddess, there is also a real-life stereotype of the bisexual woman as confused or "just experimenting." And yet bisexuality itself is difficult to define. Does being bisexual mean you actually have sex with both men and women on a regular basis, or does it merely mean that you identify as being bisexual?

It's easy to assume we know what a bisexual is, but when you try to define it (even for yourself) it can often prove quite difficult. Most folks think that if you like boys *and* girls, either you like one a bit better than the other or you must be ready to take on all comers. Others think that to be a bisexual woman means that you have a 50/50 split of men and women in your erotic life. (I, for one, don't have a chart by my bed so that I can easily check off "guy" or "girl" right after I come, to keep my Bisexual Membership intact.)

But those assumptions hint at a larger stereotype about bisexual women: Bisexuals are often considered disdainfully as having no taste—liking everything, or having too much appetite (again, liking everything). Not everyone seems to think that having the cake and eating it is cute.

When I first came out as bi, I thought that my chances of dating would double. This didn't happen. In fact, many of the lesbians I met wouldn't date me, while the guys wanted to see if they could get into a threeway with me. I felt as if potential lovers thought I couldn't be trusted to be true to either gender—because I liked both. Needless to say, this wasn't what I was hoping for.

Are bisexual women really the confused gourmands people think we are? As *we* sometimes think we are? As the stories in this book show, confusion is one thing that isn't part of our identity. This book shows sexually confident women and men having red-hot experiences with one or more lovers, women watching their bisexual male partners get off with another man, and lesbians watching their wives get fucked by a man. In this book, as in the ideal world, anything goes.

A few stories in this book fall into those stereotyped categories I mentioned before, yet they are not here as "token" stories. They are superbly written, hot, and, more importantly, *real*. I am happy to say that the stories in this book are also supremely original. Many of them don't even dwell on the fact that the authors or characters are bisexual—they are just sexual, the "bi" simply becoming two extra letters, like a "Mr." or a "Ms." They don't really change the essence of who you are.

The stories range from wickedly dark and disturbing ("Scenes from Thailand," "Night on Twelfth Street") to salaciously funny ("The Year of Fucking Badly," "On the Care and Feeding of White Boys"). Some, like "Triptych" and "Hair Club for Bisexuals," are essay-like pieces that lyrically explore bisexual relationships. "Thwack!" has a polyamorous phone sex operator juggling two relationships, "Party of One" fulfills a lesbian's fantasy with a special surprise, and "Surrender Dorothy" is a playful romp about coming out. "The Devil Is a Squirrel," "Full Service," "Leaving the Past," and "Go" take gender bending to a delicious new level.

I hope that, bi, straight, gay—or whatever you are—these stories will turn you on. I hope they'll show you what we, as bisexual women, are really thinking. I had a wonderful time editing this anthology, and I'm happy that we finally have our own place on the bookshelves.

Now can I please have my cake?

Cara Bruce
San Francisco
July 2001

Triptych

Helena Settimana

My friend Lynette and I are lying on our beds in a hotel on Lancaster Gate. We can see Hyde Park across the street with its massive, winter-naked oaks standing like wild-armed sentries. The room has red velvet drapes and gold-and-red flocked wallpaper. I suspect it is supposed to look sumptuous, but the effect is more like a second-rate whorehouse. It is raining outside, and I have been watching the beetle-black cabs and a mounted policeman passing along the slick street. I am telling her seriously that I will kill myself if I ever lose "it" before I am married. Lynette looks at me like I have three heads. She has dark-rimmed, cat-green eyes that open wider in disbelief, but she is too wise or too dumbstruck to say anything. I just might be the last virgin in my senior year, but it is all too much to absorb, so I vow self-death as an antidote to the roil inside me, brought on by the fact that a boy I have met on this March Break excursion has stuck his muscular tongue in my mouth and provoked a hormonal crisis. I rushed to brush my teeth, but felt helpless to brush away the throb that lingered between my legs. The feeling is potent and threatens to overwhelm. Death is a limited solution.

He is anxious to please, this boy, and anxious to advance his cause. He has unruly jet-black hair and pale, freckled, Scottish skin. He has been a figure-skater, is muscular and lean, and comes from another school, stuck on the same itinerary. Craig follows me, alternating puppyish flirtation with macho posturing. On the night after we meet we all go out to a play and in the dark he gently draws his thumb across my palm and ventures a hand on my thigh. My breath is suspended. I feel incapable of rising to my feet at the end of the first act, slick and damp. He remains seated for a while after I excuse myself to find the bathroom. My friends are watching me closely. To this day I don't remember the name of the play.

I try to remember my vow.

He sees me to my hotel room door, where Lynette has disappeared discreetly inside. He kisses with his tongue again and ventures pressing himself, hard, into my belly. Panicked, I wiggle a goodnight, but the next day, and the next, my resolve begins to unravel in this miasma of newfound passion. Still, I allow him no room to go beyond.

On the tenth day we sit together riding the plane home. As the lights are dimmed he calls the flight attendant for a blanket, and wraps me discreetly beside him. The imaginary barrier is drawn between us and the rest of the world, and in this seclusion his hands wander to my breasts and carefully fondle me between my legs. Craig has taken my hand and guided it to him. I feel him hard—the first time I have ever touched a boy, a man, there. If anyone is aware of what we are doing, it goes unchallenged and our fondling continues, unchecked. When one finger slips beneath the scalloped edges of my panties, my breath catches again. I know he can't "go all the way," and so I let him slide one sturdy finger inside of me, opening my legs and pushing my hips onto his hand before sudden panic strikes again. The exploration ends. When we emerge from our hiding place, I feel the eyes of other passengers on us. They know! Somehow I feel triumphant.

I hold him at arm's length. My parents love him, adore him, trust him. They retire and leave us alone one night. He succeeds in putting his cock in my mouth. Weeks later he tells my friends, in front of me, that we are getting married but we will live together first. He hasn't mentioned this to me. It is the beginning of the end. I can't imagine settling for one man right now when this wicked new world is waiting to be discovered. I find I have a cruel heart. Just to make sure, I fuck the next guy I meet.

I'm still alive.

• • •

Leigh is standing beside the window in a cheap hotel room in Victoria. He has carried my luggage in from the curb and up two flights of stairs. I was not anticipating the Ritz, but perhaps something more on the measure of the hotel by the park. This is closer to a flophouse and is fortunately only a stopgap until I can find an acceptable room of my own. The hotel seems to crawl with the dregs of London: whores and pimps and pushers. I wonder how I am mixed in with them, and remind myself that it is only a temporary thing and that lodging here, unlike home, is exorbitant. I am a poor student and I did not book this part ahead. The heater hangs askew on the wall, broken wires dripping out, the victim of a previous tenant. The door is missing from the wardrobe, and extra linens are tossed carelessly inside. I don't want to look closely at them.

I have put aside my life to be here—to see if this is the man I want for keeps. I am now being dragged slowly into this sagging, creaking bed, stripped of my clothing, jewelry, underthings. For a while I feel as if I have come home and I collapse

3

under his weight, grateful for the warmth and familiarity of his body. He smells good, his mouth burns on me, his teeth rake the fine surface of my skin. I finger the crucifix around his neck and bend, push up into him.

The whores are fighting in the street. It's distracting me from coming. Eventually, Leigh sidles to the window to watch the show. He's blue-gray-black-and-white-TV-colored in the streetlight, bronze lined with silver. He seems distant. When he sees the management toss an unpaying visitor out into the road, he hastily dresses and leaves with a promise to return in the morning.

Early in the morning, he comes to my room and takes his sweet everlovin' time pulling the rings from my fingers, then the blouse, the slacks, the snappy bits of bra and panty off me, and lays me down tender as you like, and rubs all of the red marks out of my skin. He makes me cry out and whisper, "I love you," and when he has finished he gets this sad look on his face and says, "I'm sorry," and "It's over," and walks out, just like that—out into the dirty street. He told me that he has reconciled with his wife. Suddenly I see I am at home in this place after all.

From a phone box in the road I call Mireille in Islington and ride the train underground, walk the warren of alleys and roads that lead to her basement flat, and cry at her door as if bereft of life.

His wife. I can't believe it.

Mireille is good at serving tea and sympathy to me but is merciless with Leigh and pronounces a hex upon his cock for good measure. This makes me laugh a bit.

She says, "He will never be the same after this, but what does not kill you will make you stronger, and you will be very powerful indeed." I am giggling and hiccoughing sobs at the same time.

I've been dreaming every time I sleep. Mireille tries to rub the red marks out of my eyes, after I tell her about the rotten heel.

Mireille kisses my swollen eyelids, my mouth, down the side of my neck, draws me backward into her body with arms that are deceptively strong. I am paralyzed with shock, then eased by resignation, then loosened by desire. The glossy dark hair that curled out from under her cotton shorts shocked me into arousal—so did the tribbles of hair that peeked from under her arms. Weak, weak, I feel weak. She says, "How could he make you feel bad, how could he? He deserves to be shot."

I find myself propped like a broken doll on her hand, desperately twisting my leather-brown, nubby nipples while she moans over the three fingers I had managed to slip inside that sopping mouth.

The sound of my breath caught in the air sounds rasping, ragged. It hangs in the dark like frozen vapor emitted on a winter's night: small crystals of ice colliding. The noise is shattering in the tiny room. I am afraid that if I look on the floor I will see bits of my orgasm lying in jagged pieces: an *A* here, an *O* there. Curls of *G*'s and fragments of *F*'s. I fear we'll waken the neighbors. The sound has brought me to consciousness: my insides clasping frantically, the sharp images in my mind are shredded by wakefulness. I resolve not to panic.

Mireille rolls over, nuzzling her face into the pillow. What can I say? I feel different, new—not exactly fixed. It is too soon for that.

I think I shall never return.

• • •

The woman sprawled on the settee is staring at Jack. She looks like a young Melina Mercuri—brassy dyed-blonde hair with black roots and a single eyebrow. I look away. If the one we find looks like a Greek, it had better be like Irene Papas— my idea of a goddess. Jack is looking the other way at this leggy sylph of a thing with golden-brown hair and a dimple that makes her look a bit like Kirk Douglas, if Douglas were a woman and a delicate, skinny one at that. The dimple drops her eyes—not her, either.

It's a dare. He's got me teetering into this place on dangerous heels. I'm still madly in love. It's our tenth anniversary, and all he wants is to live his fantasy at last. We have been together so long that in the moment it seems not only safe, but exciting. I am to find an agreeable partner, ignoring the boys on the way. Jack is an adventurer, though he likes me all to himself.

In the end I spy a golden gazelle of a girl sitting in a dark corner, watching. She has a purple slash of a mouth. Jack presses himself into my ass before sending me off to broach the topic. I buy her a drink, light her cigarette, drop a strap off my shoulder, swing my pointed shoe with studied nonchalance, brush her arm as if by accident. Then she says, "Are you coming on to me?" and I have to tell her yes, and wait for her eyes to shutter, but they burn instead with a kind of smoky light and it is OK. We sit in the shadows, her skirt hiked a bit, my hand exploring the juncture of her legs. She pushes herself on my hand, her purple mouth open. She says her name is Amira. She is Kenyan and speaks with a trilling, exotic timbre to her clipped colonial English.

Jack appears like an apparition, his cock veiled in the linen of his trousers. I whisper the invitation to her and wait again for her to say no, but her mouth opens in a tiny *O* and she nods. Jack calls for our coats and leads us to the curb, hails a cab. I watch the furtive glances of the driver in the rear-view mirror as we sit flanking our new friend, probing hands on her thighs, teeth on her neck, tongues in her ears. She massages Jack's cock, and a stain begins to bleed through the fabric of his pants. I am so hot that I am out of body.

He pays the driver, who looks a little bit disappointed at our departure. Our hotel is a good one this time, decorated in dark wood and forest green, brass, Chinese vases. Amira is like a miracle shining naked on the bed. I've gently parted her lips, pulled the mouth of her sex open. She is tidy, neat, her hair trimmed, her lips understated—the color of aubergine. I wonder if she has been clipped a bit, but it's hard to tell. Seawater oozes from her pink interior.

I think of Mireille's strong arms as I pull her back into my body, laying her on top of me, stroking her blackberry nipples, brushing her belly while Jack searches for her teeny clit with his tongue. She rolls off me and offers her ass to him, pulling intently on my breast, nuzzling down into the thatch between my legs.

He fucks her. This is not exactly in the plan, at least not the one he shared with me. I'm aroused, overcome, transported by this fantasy into one of my own. I am nowhere, I am everywhere, I am he, and I am she. I inhabit their bodies and think and feel for them, make them do my bidding. She's so tiny—narrow and almost adolescent-looking—vulnerable. I offer help: help to hold her down, to spread her legs, to penetrate her. I never feel what she feels, only what he feels as she twists and moans and flails narrow avian arms and legs while he buries himself into her with force. His cock, shiny with latex and juice, is thicker than her wrist and he holds her over his lap, facing me, making sure I see as she jerks like a meat marionette on him. When they come I come too, my hand cramming my quivering hole. Jack is staring me in the eye. He whispers, "I'm the luckiest man in the world."

He may be right.

Double Down
Esther Haas

Once upon a time there was a place called Las Vegas, where nothing was quite what it seemed to be. Venice wasn't really Venice. Paris wasn't really Paris. It was all just an expensive, elaborate façade to convince you that you were in New York or ancient Egypt or someplace, anyplace, and all the while the casinos had their hands planted deep in your pockets. All the Elvises weren't really *the* Elvis, and most of the marriages made in Las Vegas weren't really till death do they part. Reality, in Las Vegas, was always up for grabs.

Karen, when she married Greg in the Little White Chapel, wasn't quite what she seemed to be, either. During the ten months they'd known each other, she hadn't bothered to tell him that, though he was indeed the only man in her life, there were women. Quite a *few* women.

She hadn't meant anything nefarious by her silence on that score. Greg was an agreeable enough dolt, sexy even, if you liked handsome, broad-shouldered ex-college athletes with big dicks, which Karen did. And they'd grown to be quite fond of one another, and Greg had a fair amount of money. So why complicate matters?

They were staying at the Bellagio, in a room with a good view of the fountains that danced around to music. Everything about it reeked of luxury. Class for sale. Bob, the rather hunky bellhop, had been as obsequiously attentive as a butler on a *Masterpiece Theatre* show.

"You didn't tell me you liked to gamble," Karen said on the third morning.

"Yeah, well, I do," Greg said. "But don't worry about it, honey. I don't bet very much. I promise." And he gave her a kiss. She liked the kiss, but she wished he wouldn't call her "honey"—it reminded her, grimly, of her parents.

At the breakfast buffet, he gave her another kiss and asked her, "You wouldn't mind my spending another couple of hours at the tables, would you?"

And Karen said that was quite all right. Which it was, seeing as how Greg had just finished eating her, and eating her well, before they'd left the room. She's been padding around in her bra and panties when he pushed her playfully down onto the bed, pulled her panties off, and started licking at her pussy. Most of the men Karen had fucked had wanted blowjobs, and she gave them expertly, taking their hard-ons deep into her throat, nursing the sperm up the shaft. But when it came time to return the favor, most of the guys had seemed uninterested, inept, or both. Not Greg, though. He was enthusiastic, as gung ho as most of the women she'd slept with, and he knew how to tease her clit with his teeth till she was sopping wet. Karen got *very* wet.

He'd been perfectly attentive to her, fucking her with his tongue, licking and sucking until she arched and moaned. And though Greg's bulky dick was stiff and throbbing, her offer to return the favor was politely turned down. "No, honey, I just wanted to make you feel good. Don't worry about me," Greg said, as he stuffed himself back into his pants. What could you do about a prize like him? Refuse him a few hands of blackjack?

"You go gamble, Greg," she said, taking one last bite of blueberry crepe, "and I'll go shopping." They had a joint platinum AmEx card, and Karen fully intended to give it a workout before they headed back to St. Louis.

"I'm not sure where I'm going to play. Meet you back in the room in time for lunch?" Perfect.

She went up the Strip to Caesar's. It was her new favorite place to shop. Maybe the shops weren't as exclusive as those at Bellagio or Mandalay Bay, but the whole indoor mall was like a Disneyfied version of Ancient Rome. It was deception on a grand scale, and Karen knew just enough about Roman history to imagine herself as some really wicked Roman—say, Messalina, or Caligula's sister. It made shopping for handbags a lot more fun.

She was perusing designer lingerie when she saw her: a Eurasian woman with a beautiful face, an incongruously spiky haircut, and big breasts (a silicone job, no doubt). It took the woman just a second to notice that Karen was staring at her. She pulled a black lace teddy from the rack, held it up in front of her, and smiled. "Like it?"

Karen did, a lot. "You look good," she said.

"I know," the woman said with a smile. "My name's Dru." She lowered the teddy so that Karen could see her forefinger tracing lazy circles on her breast.

Karen could feel that funny little tightening between her legs. "Want to go for a walk?"

"Where you staying?"

"Bellagio."

"Then let's go there." She looked, unmistakably, at Karen's wedding band. "Problem?"

"Not for the next hour or so."

"Then let's go."

"I'm a showgirl," Dru had said in the taxi on the way back to Bellagio.

"No kidding!"

"Yeah, a show called 'Le Fling.' One of the last big old-style Vegas shows left. Everything these days is overpriced magicians or French acrobats." She put a hand on Karen's thigh and started massaging. The cab driver didn't seem to notice, though Karen almost wished he did. "You should see me in my wig."

"Or out of your clothes."

The driver's head gave a little jerk, though he had, no doubt, heard a lot worse.

"Yes," said Dru. "Out of my clothes."

The room had already been made up, so there wouldn't be the maid to contend with. Karen threw the security lock. "That looks heavy," she said, as Dru unslung her big shoulder bag.

"It's my bag of tricks," she said. "I think you'll be amused." Standing very close to Karen, she took off her little white jacket, pulled her tank top over her head. Her tits were, indeed, lovely—shapely, large, but not grotesquely over-amped. Perfect. Karen reached out and stroked their warmth. Dru pressed herself against the other woman, parting her lips, kissing Karen's mouth, softly at first, exploring with her tongue, then biting down on Karen's lower lip until she flinched. Her hand wandered down to the crotch of Karen's taupe linen slacks, rubbing her cunt till she could feel moisture seeping through the thin fabric.

"Your husband?" Dru whispered.

"Don't worry about my husband. What's in that bag of yours?" Karen was stripping down gracefully.

"Turn around and get on the bed. On all fours."

Naked except for her high heels—just like in a porn movie!—Karen did as Dru commanded. Her flesh quivered. Then, moments later, she felt it, a cockhead penetrating her wet slit from behind.

"Oh, God," the newlywed moaned. "Let me see it. Please. Let me see you."

Dru pulled out and backed off. She was so beautiful naked, and from her thighs, secure in a harness, rose a curved dildo, colored in swirls of bright pink and lavender.

Karen swiveled around on the king-size bed and wrapped her lips around the silicone dick. She hadn't sucked Greg's dick this morning, but she would suck Dru's. When she'd slid it all the way down her throat, Dru's well-manicured hands pressed on the back of her head. The showgirl thrust into her mouth until she gagged.

"Enough of that. I'm going to fuck you, Mrs. Whoever-you-are. I'm going to fuck you till you come."

And then Karen was on her back, on the edge of the bed, her legs over Dru's shoulders as the dildo slid inside her. Dru's cock felt so good up her cunt. Karen reached up with one hand to squeeze Dru's dark nipple, her other hand homing in on her own clit. And at that very moment, the loudspeakers outside the hotel started blasting out Frank Sinatra: "Luck Be a Lady Tonight." Karen turned her head to look out the window; the fountains in front of Bellagio were dancing to Sinatra, shooting high into the air. Karen's fingers moved faster and faster against her swollen clit. The fountains shot even higher. Across the street, the faux–Eiffel Tower hovered in the hot Vegas air. Karen tightened, thrust, and, with something between a scream and a sigh, she came.

When she'd caught her breath, she managed to say, "Oh, God, please let me lick you—please, Dru."

The willowy woman with the big tits backed away and

undid the harness. The dildo was double headed, and the shaft she drew from inside herself was dripping wet. Karen dove onto Dru's smooth, shaved cunt, sucking and licking at the woman's swollen clit. She reached around, stroking and grabbing at Dru's silken butt.

"Oh, holy fuck, that's good, baby."

And Karen knew just what to do, her mouth working hard, hitting all the right spots, till the tingle between Dru's legs became an unstoppable force.

"Oh my fucking *God,* baby!" She came. Karen's flushed face was soaking wet.

When they'd both recovered, Karen went into the bathroom to wash up. The room was large and sumptuous, the mark of Las Vegas Luxury.

"How long will you be here?" Dru called from the next room.

"Two more days. We're leaving early, the day after tomorrow."

"Can I see you again? Tomorrow morning?"

Karen walked back into the bedroom. Dru was pulling on her little white jacket.

"I'd love that, only I'm not sure about coming here to the room. I don't know what my...husband will be up to."

"How about if we meet up at Caesar's again? Same shop, say ten-thirty?" Dru hoisted her big bag onto her shoulder.

"Ten-thirty it is."

They kissed, gently but passionately, and Karen, in just bra, panties, and heels, felt herself getting excited again. Dru slipped her hand into her bra, cupped her breast.

"You'd better get going. Greg will be...."

"Till tomorrow morning, babe." And Dru was gone.

The sex that night between Karen and Greg was great, explosively great—Greg tonguing her cunt and asshole, then plowing his big dick into her as she gasped and writhed. On a whim, she licked her fingertips, reached around to Greg's asshole, and rubbed the puckered flesh. Within seconds, her husband shot off inside her.

They went to see the Bellagio's show, "O"—more French acrobats—then to the top of the Stratosphere Tower for a nightcap, all Las Vegas glittering, phony-but-beautiful, far below. In the cab that took them back down the Strip, Karen snuggled up to Greg. She'd seldom been so happy. And there was still the next morning with Dru to look forward to.

"How'd you do gambling this morning?" she asked.

"Pretty well. I actually came out a bit ahead."

"You want to gamble one last time tomorrow?"

"You don't mind, honey?"

"Not at all. I'd like to go back to Caesar's shops. There was something I saw there that I really liked."

Karen was excited. Greg was safely tucked away in some casino or other for the morning, and she was looking forward to Dru and her big bag of tricks. She got to the store early, trying to seem interested in the underwear for sale. Ten-thirty came and went, then 10:45. No Dru. Ten minutes later, she gave up. Either something had come up, or Dru had lied. Either way, she was going to head back to the Bellagio.

"Have you found anything you like?" the salesgirl purred.

"Actually, yes. I'll take this." She held out the black lace teddy that Dru had held the day before: a souvenir. And Greg would like her in it.

She went to the counter, opened her little purse.

"Anything wrong, madam?"

The platinum American Express card was gone. Karen rummaged through everything. Twice. No, it was gone. She might, just *might* have lost it, but....

Yesterday! When she was in the bathroom. Dru had ripped her off. The bitch. The scheming, beautiful bitch.

"Do you know," Karen asked the salesgirl, "where a show called 'Le Fling' is playing?"

" 'Le Fling'? No such show."

"Are you certain?"

"I'm sure. Never heard of it."

Karen rushed out, through the immensity of Caesar's Forum Shops, past the Trojan Horse in front of the toy store, past the show where, amidst flames and thunder, Atlantis was sinking to the bottom of the sea.

The cab crawled through the clot of a midday traffic jam on the Strip. She was wishing she'd phoned American Express from the store, cancelled the card right away. Oh well, if she ever got back to her room, there would be time to phone, to wait for Greg, to make up some story about how she lost the card. What he didn't know wouldn't hurt him. Karen had been a fool, but at least she'd gotten fucked, and fucked well, out of the deal.

Finally back at the hotel, she hurried through the lobby, beneath the multicolored glass sculpture, past the business-people, the couples, the gawkers. Elevator up. She had to take a pee. She slipped the card into the door's electronic lock.

The room was semidark, the blackout curtain having been pulled nearly shut. It took her eyes a second to adjust. It took her mind another second to register what was going on in the bed.

Greg, her husband, was lying there naked, legs in the air, being fucked. Fucked up the ass by Bob, the hunky bellhop. They'd frozen, were both looking her way.

Karen didn't know what to do. She might be a slut, but she was a slut who didn't believe in the double standard.

"Honey...." Greg's voice sounded strangled.

"You boys using a condom?"

Bob the bellhop, ever eager to please, pulled out of her husband's ass. Despite the dim light, she could she his thick little cock was wrapped securely in latex.

"Well then, go ahead. You mind if I watch?"

"You can join in if you want, ma'am," said Bob the bell-hop, politely. The service at this hotel certainly *was* first rate.

"Thanks," Karen said, but I'd hate to intrude." She reached inside her pants, slid two fingers between her cunt lips, stroking as she watched her husband getting plowed up the butt. It was exciting, watching her husband taking it up the ass, thrashing and groaning and finally shooting cum all over his lean belly. It was exciting when Bob pulled out, peeled off the rubber, stroked his cock until his cum shot in big, wet arcs, some of it landing in Greg's hair. It was exciting enough to make her come, too. It was exciting enough for her to start making plans; after all, Dru wasn't the only one who could wear a strap-on.

And they lived—Karen and Greg and Karen's girlfriends and Greg's boyfriends and Karen's big, expensive bag of toys—happily ever after.

The Smell of It

Thea Hillman

It's late when Casey and I get home, and we don't have the energy to fuck. So we masturbate for each other. She starts touching herself, but she's shy and she's worried that it's going to take her a long time. After a few silent minutes of her touching her pussy and me stroking her thighs, she turns her head on the pillow and says, "Talk to me." I feel a preliminary performance-anxiety-laden, oh-no-I've-got-to-come-up-with-something-good panic, but then a picture of Casey working out swims into my head. Now, I've never seen her work out, but she's a firefighter and in EMT training to be a paramedic and has to stay strong, so I start, "You're at the gym doing leg presses." And I don't really know what leg presses are, but her legs are extremely muscular, so I go with it. "The gym is full of men, but they let you use the machines because you're as big as they are." And it's true: Casey's a gangly six feet and carries herself like a dude. Public restrooms are hell for her because most people she encounters think she's a guy. Her uniform of jeans, tight jogging bra, T-shirt, and Elmo baseball cap doesn't help either. I've seen her called *son* at a rodeo, and even at a sex party one time a woman squealed, "There's a man in here!" when Casey entered the bathroom to change. So fantasies of her passing or competing as a boy—teenage at that—come fast and furious for me.

"You're doing leg presses," I say. I'm stroking the muscles as I talk about them, "and your quads strain against your gray shorts as you do your first set of reps. Dots of sweat start showing through your shirt and the sweat beads, roll down between your breasts, tickling you before they soak your bra. Your energy builds as you start to exert yourself. It's almost sexual, and you focus all of it in your legs." As I'm talking, Casey's fingers start to move a little faster, and I realize that it's not just passing as a man that's both difficult and fun for her, but also that the energy between her and other men is hot for her. And then I remember the story she told me about her coworker at the firehouse.

When we started dating, Casey told me about Mike, the other new firefighter in the station. They spent a lot of time together doing the requisite grunt work between calls, and they became close friends. Like brothers, they would screw around, wrestling and roughhousing and teasing each other about girls. Mike had a girlfriend and was cool with Casey's being gay. But there was this one time that Casey told me about, when they hugged goodbye before the two-week break between shifts, that they hugged closer than usual, and Casey told me she felt Mike against her. His cock. She wasn't sure if it was hard or not, but just feeling it against her was more than she'd ever done with a guy.

"You're reaching the end of your first set," I continue. "You close your eyes with the effort, breath coming harder as your muscles push, forcing away the weights. You open your eyes and catch one of the guys watching you in the mirror, staring at the muscles that flex in your legs with each extension."

And what ensued after this quick hug with Mike was Casey telling me fantasies she had, first about hugging him, feeling him hard against her or feeling his cock against her back as he passed her in the kitchen. The fantasies progressed to her sucking his cock. I was sure that the "him fucking her" fantasy was just around the corner.

"It's funny, the guy watching your legs," I tell her, "because you don't shave and each of your muscles is well-defined, but the lines are smoother than a man's; longer, more sustained. And you know that some people notice this and some people don't, depending on what they want to see. You wonder what he thinks you are. You feel him watching you. And the quick jolt of adrenaline tells you it's sexual, the heat and wet of working out."

Although I knew that Mike and Casey were probably never going to even kiss each other, I also knew that something was opening in Casey, something hot and deep, a desire free of fear. I knew that she was curious enough and brave enough that someday she might play with this desire, maybe even satisfy it.

"The heat and wet combine with the liquids of arousal. Your breasts and palms are sweaty, the crevice between your pussy and thigh soaked." At this point, I'm getting that the words *wet* and *sweat* are working for Casey, so I sprinkle them liberally through my narrative. "The high from pumping your muscles and feeling the strength of your body, the cool wetness of your shirt sticking to you, the sheen of sweat on your legs, along with these guys noticing you, mixes until you're not sure which is which and it doesn't matter because all the energy helps you finish your second set. You've got one more, and you try to slow your breathing down, gather yourself, and then begin again. You narrow your focus, watching your own body now, marveling at the sweat that highlights your thighs and calves. You unclench your hands from the bench and slide your hands down your legs as they work, feeling yourself as your muscles contract and expand, and you grunt softly with each exertion."

Casey's breath comes faster now, her arm tightening with the effort of rubbing her clit in fast, wet circles.

"Without even looking up, you notice that a few more guys have stopped what they're doing, standing at a machine or with free weights in their hands, just watching you. Your muscles are burning now, hurting, and you focus even more, matching your breath with the rhythm of the reps, barely noticing the other machines, the men close by, the swirling of other bodies, quadriceps, triceps, at this point only muscles, bulges, moving, thrusting, pushing, and then releasing. Sweat is dripping off your face, down your chest, and you're not sure if you can do the last five, but the guys are checking you out, and you can't stop now. Then something grabs your attention. It's a smell, and at first you think maybe you smell yourself, but then you realize it's coming from somewhere close by. It's the smell of guy sweat, and not just sweat, but it smells like Mike, after a fire, when all of you are exhausted and exhilarated, coming down from the high of fighting fire, and glad to be alive, strip off the layers of protective gear, get down to the wet and sweat-drenched clothes, sweat that wreaks of fear and hard work and adrenaline, pure and animal-like. And not until this minute did you realize how much the smell is part of why you love fire fighting and that the smell turns you on just as much as touching someone's cunt or the sound of a woman coming from the way you're touching her. That smell of men, and a picture of Mike stripping down the layers of his clothing, and the motion of nearby muscles is exactly what you need to get through your last set. You control your breath now, measured. You're wet and hot."

At this point, Casey moans and begins to clench next to me. "They're watching you. The sweat and heat of your effort is burning the muscles in your legs and the muscles between them. When you don't think you can push any harder, you breathe in, tasting the thick air around you," I say, and she moans again. This is the part I love—she finally stops controlling her breath, and it comes out faster now, throaty, and she's quietly but surely shuddering next to me. "You finish your last five reps with a groan. Wasted, you fall back, limp against the seatback of the bench, catching your breath, almost light-headed. Your shirt is drenched with sweat, and after a minute, you gather enough strength and stumble into the showers."

Scenes from Thailand
Rachel Resnick

Bangkok

Here we are, in another girly bar. Same, same, every night. On our way in, the *katoey* are merciless. Three of them, lounging up against the wall outside the bar.

"Ooooh," and "big boy," they say, grabbing at Gary's arms and crotch. "Show us, hunh?" One points at my tits. "Real?" Then to Gary, "Squeeze 'em. Look," and she pulls one fake tit out of her chintzy leopard print halter, grabs his arm roughly, and makes to press it there.

Gary withdraws his arm, slows, smiles, exchanges a few whispered words. The *katoey* giggle and slap Gary's butt as he walks by.

"Bye-bye," they sing, waving to me mockingly. I didn't even want to come tonight. But Gary won 2,500 *baht* playing horses and insisted. There's always a reason, and his eyes light up so when I say OK. How can I be jealous of *katoey?*

Singha beers. Itchy strobes. House music. A horseshoe-shaped stage. More slender girl-women, this time in cowgirl outfits. Sequined silver vests and cowboy hats, tooled boots, and white leather G-strings. Walker is transfixed, doesn't notice me fidgeting. I told Walker I didn't feel like coming tonight—how many girly bars do we have to go to?

In the corner is a wide-screen TV showing one scene continuously. At first I don't know what it is, think it's some psychedelic lava lamp effect, a throbbing pulse of pinks and blacks, sea anemones locked in mortal combat, an animated Rauschenberg, a mouth undergoing invasive surgery—but then I see it is an extreme close-up of a four-foot-high black cock sluicing in and out of a five-foot-high pink pussy.

I look around, embarrassed, but no one is paying any attention to me, and I realize I have never really watched porn, let alone hung out in girly bars night after night. The movement is mesmeric, and I have to steady myself from swaying with my hand on the back bar. Again I look at Walker, to anchor my vision, but he too has not moved—it is as if everything is moving repetitively or else has stopped moving altogether. The bar is undulous and wavery, with frozen parts. I realize I am soaking and it reminds me of the sensation I sometimes have when I am bleeding, that all my innards are slip-sliding down and will flush out along with the blood, leaving me gutless.

It is only with great concentration that I can tear my gaze away from the screen and join Walker in viewing the stage. We are now one gaze, Walker and I, swallowing up each and every girl—and I, for the first time, am his partner. Look, touch, take. There is always more and there is never enough and all is molten. Oceanic. I think I'm getting it.

With one look now I can pierce through the veil of manner, see desire. Everyone is want. What did the Buddhist tract say? "One must look correctly to be able to penetrate, otherwise one will see nothing." But was it meaning this? I can't remember.

A particular girl captures my attention. Instead of cowboy boots, she's wearing Doc Martens, and looks more Samoan than Thai. She is built, and attacks the pole with muscularity, climbing to the top then slowly twirling back down head first, her legs snaked around the gleaming pole, then pow, into a split, wham, into a back handspring, all meaty shimmer and steel-toed boots.

Now the girls openly eye me while the men hunched around the stage shoot me homicidal looks. It is the first time I've noticed the men hating me. Walker nudges my side.

"The girls don't like men—all those ugly drunken tourists, hitters, losers. They're into women."

He is so enjoying this. A nothing guy with red crew cut and close-set eyes actually spits in my direction.

"These men want to kill me," I say.

It's not only a revelation; it's a turn-on. I am powerful. Electric rays snake out from my fingertips and into the watery reality strobing around me.

Four Singha bottles later, not the Samoan but another girl, Suki, is grinding her soft ass up against my groin. I find myself placing my hands on her bare hips, guiding her, the fringe of her vest swaying at my fingers, the dimple of those hips softly indented and cool to the touch. She is the only girl wearing high heels—scuffed white numbers like you'd wear to a wedding and toss afterward. I want to hold Suki, keep the gnarly men away, give her a sack of American silver dollars to match her outfit.

Buzzing and ultrasensitive, I feel something shift in the air. Walker, on my left, also leaning against the back bar, has placed his hand on Suki's hip and she freezes. He slips his hand up onto her arm and I can feel the hairs rise there. *She's mine*, I want to tell him. *Don't touch*. But instead, I gently push her toward the bar so he can't see. She turns toward me, her black bangs swinging.

"Buy me a drink," she says shyly, pointedly ignoring Walker.

But it is Walker who goes to the bar, gets her a drink, some blue-colored confection.

While he is gone, I reach up and lightly brush my fingers against her tit. She's so flat. How the fuck old is she? I can't tell anyone's age at all in Thailand. She could be thirty; she could be thirteen.

They turn on the lights and the house shifts to slow-dance goodnight get-out sap.

"Let's go," I say to Walker.

I want to escape from the harshly unpleasant glare. I've had enough. But he hangs back. Suki has moved away, stands in a cluster with some of the other girls who now, in the blinding light, look incredibly young, all carrying school satchels with bionic bright flower stickers on the flaps.

"Walker," I say.

What is he waiting for? He is a different man at night, in these bars, more wired and distant. It makes me panicky, afraid I'll lose him. We move slowly toward the door, but Walker stops at the cluster, says something to Suki, who looks away. The other girls giggle. Walker rejoins me.

"I asked her to maybe come out and have a bite to eat with us or something."

"Walker, it's three A.M. I'm tired."

Suki looks uncertain, catches my eye. When she does, her eyes turn dead. In their reflection, I see a hoary-scaled reptile shedding his pink-fleshed humanoid daywear. The blush suffuses my face, but she has already turned her back to me and together with the other young girls, en masse, the many-legged, many-armed, flower-satcheled young cowgirls melt away.

Phuket

The whore's name is Bang and she has a crush on me. She is on break. Most of the girls in Delight Ship Bar are dressed in school uniforms, white ankle socks, heels. A few wear cheap synthetic dresses. Bang wears a minijumper and scuffed white pumps that are two sizes too big. Before she went on break I watched her dance. I stared at her narrow heels sliding around in the pumps that belonged to someone else, then at the sweet *V* of her shaved crotch, which kept appearing and disappearing as she wriggled against a pole in front of her. I could have stuck two fingers in that gap behind her heel. Two thick American fingers.

Bang barely reaches to my chest, and I can circle her wrists with my index finger and thumb. Bang has a friend named Bong. I prefer Bong. She is taller, curvier, more sultry, with long eyelashes and a constellation of freckles that looks like dirt over her left clavicle. Bong leans over, whispers in my ear.

"You are better looking than him," she hisses. "You should not be with him."

I like her warm breath in my ear. She squeezes my waist, then goes back on stage. Bang presses her slender hip against mine.

"Take me home," she says.

She ignores Walker. Walker who's leering, who's eyes are moist with anticipation.

Bang holds my hand as we walk through the crowded street, past carbuncled men with perfect Thai girls at their sides, girls who are bought and yet the men are proud, they walk by as if they are hot shit, this is their pretty young girl-friend and it's all real, when the truth is they hemorrhage money to pay for a whole night with these girls. What is real is the stink of Third World sewage and rot, the fry smell of cooking dough, simmering chilies, twinkly lights strung hap-hazardly everywhere, and everyone leering, me too, my face is figured by kink, and Bang's small hand is in mine.

People are watching, staring. This threesome is something a bit out of the ordinary even for the beach town of Phuket, not much, but a little, happening only every half hour instead of steadily on the second, every second. She talks to me, Bang does, about her family. She has three children. She is from

Laos. In Laos they have a very primitive counting system: one, two, three, many.... Bang wears a gold necklace and bracelet and anklet. In the shadow-pocked night they glitter against her dusky skin. Her hand is humid, meltable, but then so is everything. The world is covered in a sheen of sweat. I am in Phuket, walking hand in hand with a whore down a street back to the hotel room I share with Walker.

We sit on the bed, awkwardly. The TV is on. Time is a slinky. Time is tight coils of seconds stretching *U*-shaped over our heads, between our bodies, then collapsing with a slap. The thin bedspread is decorated with cross-country skiers. It is 90 degrees even now.

"Something to drink?" Walker says. "Orange soda?"

"Please, yes."

"Me too," I say, and Bang and I sip from the same orange soda can.

After some long minutes pass, us staring listlessly at the TV screen, Walker says to me, "Kiss her." I kiss her.

She tastes like Laos. Pungent, earthy, fetid, powerful, rank, completely foreign. I recoil. To compensate, I kiss her with more passion, brush back her silken black hair and cradle her head as if I am the man. Bang is so tiny. I want to make her come. I know whores rarely come, if ever, even though I've never been with one. I want to make her happy, and I want to turn Walker on, show him what I can do.

With her delicate frame, she's almost weightless above me, like she's floating. I remember playing airplane with my father, how his fat feet lofted me high into the air. I lift Bang, softly place her shellfish cunt against my thigh, and make her ride, deep-kissing her into an altered state. My thigh is a stallion, and her cunt is riding barebacked, shaved clean. I feel the pulsing there, a naked mouth with pursed lips, trying to speak.

As she writhes on my body, I see again an image from this afternoon: the ex-votos, those parti-colored frangipani fabrics they tie around sacred trees for blessings, undulating in the sea breeze. This is her body. Slender. Furling and unfurling. Silk-spun. I hold Bang close. She grabs a handful of my fat American tit in her tapered fingers, sucks on the nipple furiously. Maybe I am a fantasy for her, vaguely suggesting one of those fleshy babes who charges up and down the TV beach in her wet red clingsuit; perhaps it's simply my otherness that makes her wet; maybe, like she to me, I stink of the foreign, too. Maybe all those soaps and lotions, perfumes and sprays seem a kind of formaldehyde to her, and she is wondering as she searches my body, What are Americans trying to hide?

Now Bang is making little gasps. Encouraged, I become merciless; for minutes, hours, my thigh gallops against her pretty little cunt. I dare not touch that cunt, although I think about touching her the way I touch myself. But that is my private prayer, the secret communion of my own flesh and fingers. Like a bat, I blindly radar in on Bang's steady, small gasps, search for clues to take her home. Then we are grooving together on a shared plateau where foreign tongues blend, and two bodies are reborn as Siamese twins, joined at the hip of Walker's greedy gaze.

This is taking forever. Before we finish, the whole world will have rubbed its genitals into oblivion.

Pressing harshly against her cunt, I make more violent, urgent moves, wanting this to be over, wanting Bang to love me for just this moment. I crush the smooth, almost rubbery nether lips, mash them so her pubic bone clicks back and forth, and it is like I'm kneeing her in the cunt. It would take so little to damage her, and I am tempted. I hold Bang even more tenderly, shamed by my impulse, unable to imagine three children emerging from between her fragile legs. Finally Bang exhales a sharp, bestial yelp.

I am exhausted. Disgusted. Triumphant. Disoriented. It is as if I have woken from a strange claustrophobic dream and here it is, that dream. Inescapable. Her juice trembles down my thigh, her bony chest shudders against my pillowy breasts as if she were my baby. If I dared, I would pick her up and hurl her from the door of The Seagull Cottages, #7. She is old enough to fly. Bang wants to keep kissing me. Finally she asks Walker if he wants to fuck her.

"No," he says. "Nah."

He pays her at the door. Bang wants to come back tomorrow, to visit me. She wants to bring her three children to play at the beach. I say I'd love to. Bang gives me her number, kisses me shyly on the lips. When tomorrow comes, we take the train back to Bangkok.

On the train, Walker does not mention the whore, but I cannot stop thinking about the smallness of her hands, her assaultive smell, how much I loathed and cared for her at the same time—a woman I know not at all. Some other kind of currency was exchanged during that transaction. Something more valuable than *baht* was traded.

Happy Loving Couple Makes It Look So Easy

Susan Coss

"Oh...sweet...fucking...Jesus," I gasp.

"Hey-zeus, se pronuncia hey-zeus," he says as he makes those final thrusts before collapsing on top of me.

We lie entwined for a few moments. The sounds of the waves hit the shore just a few hundred yards away, nearly drowning out our heavy breathing. I relish this feeling of male weight on me, of callused hand on my breast. I allow a few minutes to pass before I begin stirring, moving him off me. He tries to hold me back, but I say, "No. No, my husband is probably beginning to wonder where I am. He gets so jealous." I marvel at how easily these words tumble out of my mouth—*my husband*. I wrap the sarong around me, tie the ends around my neck, and kiss him one last time before I leave the little cabana, home of our brief tryst.

It's just barely dark as I make my way across the pool area, up the stairs to the elevator that will take me to our room on the top floor of this hotel at the southernmost end of the Baja Peninsula. I open the door quietly, thinking Greg is asleep, but across the room I see the red tip of his cigarette.

"Well," he says, taking a long drag.

"Well what?"

"Don't play innocent. I saw you disappear with that bartender into the cabana." He stands up. "Slut, I can still smell him on you!" He jumps on the bed and begins bouncing. "Adulterer!" he screams, and I jump up to join him, laughing.

"Oh baby, I never knew adultery could feel so good." We tumble on the bed and I give him all the juicy details, loving that special friendship, that bond, that only a gay man and a bisexual woman can know.

We never intended to marry. It was actually the flight attendant's fault. By the time the plane boarded, we were already drunk. A two-hour delay and three margaritas later, we were headed south. And so when the attendant came by to take our drink order, Greg said, "A bottle of bubbly," and she asked, "Honeymooners?" Greg looked at me and then replied, "No, our one-year anniversary." He saw the question in my eyes and leaned forward to whisper, "I bet we get a free bottle."

She smiled at us, opened the bottle, and poured our glasses, sighing, "Oh, to still be so in love. On the house!" As she continued down the aisle we laughed at our ruse and drank the whole bottle, so that by the time we landed, we were firmly entrenched in our deceptive role of husband and wife.

We were running away from the never-ending February rains of San Francisco. Our melatonin-deprived bodies screaming for sun and the azure waters of the Sea of Cortez.

The concierge was patient with us, used as he must have been to drunk arrivals. He told us our room was at the back of the hotel and Greg said, "Señor, there must be a mistake, I booked an oceanfront suite."

The concierge tried to explain they were completely booked, but Greg pleaded. "But it's our anniversary, there must be something...." The man behind the desk smiled, nodded his head, and then said the only suite left was the honeymoon, which he'd give to us for just $200 extra, well below the going rate.

"For my wife, the world," and Greg took my hand and kissed it lovingly. We were high from the champagne, the lie, and the thought of our inflated stock options waiting for us back home.

Xavier took us to our room, a lovely corner suite on the top floor with a balcony, a sunken tub, and one large, king-size bed. We giggled at our new sleeping arrangement, hastening the departure of Xavier, who mistakenly sensed an amorous scene unfolding before his eyes.

We spent our days lounging by the pool, drinking tequila sunrises at 11 A.M., margaritas at 1, and piña coladas at 4. It was on the second day, into our second colada, that I leaned over to Greg and murmured, "We should have a fight. I want a tempestuous marriage."

He replied, "I think you want to get rid of me so you can get laid." He stood suddenly, knocking over the chaise longue, and yelled, "Fine, I'm leaving," winking at me as he strode by, all eyes around the pool on us.

That was how I found myself at the bar, playing the role of poor wife, Heyzeus pouring me drink after drink in sympathy as I told him in hushed tones of my husband the philanderer, my unhappiness after one year, my need for a real man. And he took it upon himself to relieve me of my sorrow for two wonderful hours in that cabana by the beach.

• • •

Greg and I dress for dinner. It is our last night in Cabo; our brief respite is coming to an end. We walk down the hill into town, holding hands. At the restaurant he buys me roses and when the waiter asks if we are honeymooners, we explain— No, un aniversario de un año. The complimentary drinks arrive. We are now used to working this anniversary thing, having been let mistakenly into the marriage club, where membership obviously has its privileges—the free dinners, the daily fruit basket at the hotel, the drinks, and, Christ almighty, the illicit sex.

"Let's go dancing," I say after dinner. "I bet we could find a gay bar."

Greg quickly says, "There is one just a couple of blocks from here."

"And you know this…how?" I ask.

"Well, you're not the only one indulging in extramarital activity, you know."

Greg leads the way, and we are disappointed when we see the line to get in. We decide to try our luck elsewhere and wander the harbor until we pass a door, and hear that undercurrent of heavy bass beat, and I notice the small, nondescript rainbow flag hanging by the entrance.

It is wall to wall boys, and as we enter I see the heads turn in our direction. There are no women to be seen. We make our way to the bar and order a round of Tecates. We find a table and Greg yells to me, "I don't know about this." I just smile back at him and kiss him on the cheek. We are soon approached by a short, balding man who sits down with us.

"I'm Max, the owner," he says, extending his hand, and we make our introductions. He wants to know how we found his club, where we are from, how long we are in town for. Greg is sitting across the table from Max and me, and lets me do all the talking. The music is so loud that I have to lean completely into Max and practically press my lips against his ear for him to hear me. Greg looks around the club, seemingly bored to anyone who doesn't know him, but I know he is cruising the clientele.

"So what are you *really* doing here?" Max says.

I pause before I answer. "Well, the truth of the matter is, Greg and I are here in Cabo for our one-year anniversary." I find that, even at this club, it's impossible to let go of the lie.

"Why a gay bar?" Max asks.

"This is a little embarrassing, but I might as well tell you." I take a breath before I continue. "It has always been my fantasy to watch Greg have sex with a man. And for my anniversary present, he has finally consented." We both look over at Greg, who is quite ignorant of what I have just told Max.

"Really."

"Really. But he's a little freaked out by it, and I think he just needs to be seduced, coaxed into it. He's never done anything like this before."

"Really." I can see I have Max hooked.

"Do you know that man standing at the bar by himself?" And Max turns to see where I am looking. "He's quite attractive." I know Greg's type: tall and dark, to balance his blond Midwestern good looks.

"Ah, Roberto. I think I might be able to help you out here." Max excuses himself.

Greg smiles at me and yells, "Having fun?" I nod my head and out of the corner of my eye see Max talking to Roberto. They look over at us and Roberto waves. I wave back. "Hey, do you see that guy at the bar, the one talking to Max? He's pretty hot." Again I nod my head in agreement, trying to hide my smile.

Max heads back to the table, with Roberto in tow. They both sit down and Max introduces Roberto to us. Roberto extends his hand to Greg and as they shake, he holds Greg's hand longer than necessary and looks him straight in the eye as he says, "Mucho gusto." I almost fall out of my chair as Greg turns bright red and begins to stammer, while Roberto launches into full-press charm mode.

We have a few more rounds on Max, and then Roberto says, "Can I give you a lift back to the hotel?"

I feign exhaustion and say, "Greg, honey, I think I *am* a little tired." The three of us leave the bar, and I walk between them, holding their hands. We climb into his car and I tell Roberto we are at the Terra del Fin.

"Bueno, nice place," Roberto says with a smile.

I touch his arm. "Roberto, you should come back to our room and see the view. It is truly one made for love." He agrees. Greg is silent in the back of the car. I am sure he hates me at the moment, wondering why I would torture him like this.

We are outside the door to our room when I say, "I think I'll go get some ice. You boys make yourselves comfortable."

I return moments later and stand hesitantly at the door. I hadn't really thought far enough in advance to know what I would do at this moment. Do I play the voyeuristic wife? I turn the handle and walk into a dark room. I see the outline of their bodies on the balcony, the moon shining bright behind them. They are standing shoulder to shoulder, and I feel my nipples harden against my bra. I pour two drinks and walk out to join them.

Greg is visibly nervous with my presence. We look at one another, trying to gauge whether or not our "marriage" is ready for this next step. Roberto moves closer to him and touches his arm. I take Greg's hand and place it over Roberto's crotch. I can feel his hard-on through the rough, cotton material of his pants, and I kiss Roberto on his lips. I pull away just as Roberto tries to squeeze my ass, saying, "No, I am just going to watch."

I see Greg's hand cupping Roberto, and I guide Roberto's hand toward Greg's crotch. He is hard as well. Roberto leans in and kisses Greg, at first softly but then more passionately. Greg's hand moves from Roberto's crotch to his ass, pulling him closer. Their bodies press into each other, hard cock to hard cock. Their tongues continue to dance. They are so consumed that they have become oblivious to my presence.

My role of wife instigating sexplay is complete. I clear my throat to interrupt their moment. I lean over to Greg, kiss him on the lips, and whisper, "Happy anniversary."

My nipples ache as Roberto and Greg again begin kissing softly, and then with a voraciousness I have never seen. My hand slides over my breasts and down to my cunt. I am wet, I am hot, and I am completely forgotten by the two men in front of me.

I leave the balcony, and then the room. I head down the hall, hearing the door close behind me.

I decide to go to the bar to figure out how I'll occupy myself for the next few hours. I see from the top of the stairs that Heyzeus is working the bar again, and it's not too busy. I sit down in front of him, and he is surprised I am alone, though not disappointed.

"Tu esposo?" he asks.

I drop my head, shake it slowly, and pretend to dab my eyes with the lime wedge I have in my hand. When I lift my head back up, I have tears in the corners, and I say, "Oh Heyzeus, esta borracho—stinking, falling-down borracho." And he takes my hand and spits out, "Your husband is *mierda*." I shake my head in agreement and smile to myself, knowing the next few hours will pass just fine.

Night on Twelfth Street
Marilyn Jaye Lewis

In the half-light before dawn, the double bed jostles me from sleep, shaking with a distinct rhythm, like riding the double L train from First Avenue into Canarsie. It's Manny jerking off again. Lately he seems to need this furtive sexual stimulation before dashing off to work at the last minute—strictly solitary sex is what he's after. Sex that doesn't involve me, that lands his jism in a T-shirt, the T-shirt winding up in the tangle of sheets for me to discover later when I'm alone. And I'm the one who he says is possessed by demons. Nympho demons, the kind of demons his aunt, the Mother Superior, warned him about when he was a teenaged Catholic boy in Buffalo. He's only twenty now, six years younger than me.

Manny came into my life almost as an afterthought, like an unwanted conception late in life, and I can't figure out how to get him to leave. Whenever I suggest it might be time for him to move out of my little hellhole on East Twelfth Street and find a home of his own, he punches me repeatedly and starts smashing dishes that are irreplaceable heirlooms from my favorite dead grandmother.

The one nice thing about this Catholic boy, though, is that he's so hung up on his Catholic upbringing that he's psychologically incapable of coming in a girl's mouth. I can suck him until the proverbial cows come home and never have to swallow so much as a drop of his spunk. The sin of wasting his seed in this specific way weighs heavy on his conscience. But all the other sins have found a home in him.

His soul is blacker than tar, mostly because his mind is so fucked up. Let's face it, he's too inquisitive to be Catholic, but he was raised by a father who beat him regularly, who alternated between using a leather belt on his ass and bare fists on his face, and a mother who was a sister to the top nun. It's left a seemingly permanent schism in his psyche. Four months ago, he was a straight-A student at the university, studying to be an architect. Now he works as a ticket-seller in a gay porno movie house over by the West Side Highway. It's run by the mob and it's the only gay porno house left with a backroom for sex in these days of AIDS.

There are a lot of things about Manny that don't make sense if you weren't raised Catholic, which I wasn't. Still, I've heard him babble on enough these last couple of months to put the pieces together. He started out a trusting little boy with a good heart, but dogma has doomed him to a destiny of sociopathic perversion. I try to tell him to get over it already, that this isn't Buffalo anymore, it's New York City. Here he can be whoever he wants to be. Sometimes he listens to me intently and makes love to me in the dark as if he's starving for a sanctity he believes he can find in a woman's body. Other times the black cloud rolls over his face and the fist flies out, connecting with my cheekbone.

It was never my intention to save Manny from himself, just to lead him to the vast waters of the variety of human experience and let him drink. But the variety proved to be too much for his conscience. Sometimes, without my knowing it, the things I'd want to do to him in bed would push him over the edge, and instead of succumbing to orgasm I'd end up dodging his fists. Lately I don't have the strength to wave so much as a white flag. I'm reduced to trying to read his mind and staying the hell out of his way.

I like it when Manny's at work. I like the fact that the movie house is open around the clock and that his shift in the little ticket-taker's booth is twelve hours long. It doesn't matter a bit to me that he's back to doing blow, either. Even though it makes me spit each time I discover he's stolen my hard-earned money from my wallet, I'd rather he spent all night in the horseshoe bar on East Seventh Street without me. Then he's more likely to skulk around the Lower East Side looking for more blow at four o'clock in the morning, increasing the risk of landing himself in the Tombs again. He hates the violence of the Tombs. He's come out of there sobbing. But having him locked in that mad monkey house is preferable to having his unpredictable rage lying next to me in bed.

I wish I could get him to give me back my key. I wish I could afford a locksmith to change the lock on my door. I'm going to find a way to get him out of here. I'm going to do it soon. Ruby's band is back from their tour of northern Africa and Marseilles. She's trying to quit junk again, which means she wants to have sex with me. It's her pattern, and I've come to count on it. I love her so much it's scary.

I can't explain why I love Ruby. We have next to nothing in common. We don't seek the same highs. We don't like the same music. When we're lying in bed together we run out of things to say. I don't hang out in dyke bars like she does. I don't wear black leather. Even our tricks are from different worlds. I don't venture into the park after midnight to support a heroin habit. A cheap handjob in the shadows is not for me.

My tricks are uptown men who shoot their spunk in broad daylight. Restaurateurs, or entrepreneurs, wealthy men whose emptiness is too complex for what can be gotten in ten minutes at twenty bucks a pop behind some bushes. Ruby wouldn't fare well in those uptown luxury apartments. She's not OK with being handcuffed. She doesn't own a pair of high heels. Holding onto a man's dick in the dark is the limit of what she can stomach. Pussy is where her heart lies.

The first time I made out with Ruby, in a toilet stall in CBGB's, I didn't know she was on junk. I only knew she was a good kisser, which was why I'd followed her into the stall. We didn't do anything wild in there; we didn't unzip our jeans or pull up our T-shirts—we just kissed. But kissing Ruby was enough to make me fall in love. Her face close to mine like that, her brown eyes closing when our lips touched, her dark hair brushing lightly against my face, then the soft groans in her throat as our bodies rubbed against each other in that suggestive rhythm. Only now do I understand why she seemed to be in slow motion. It wasn't some trance of Eros; it was the gold rushing through her veins.

I didn't want to compete with the junk. I wanted the whole girl. When I told Ruby that, we didn't kiss again for a year. I blew my money that year on the gypsies on Avenue C. Mostly on the youngest girl, the fourteen-year-old with the stray eye. I paid her to hold my hand in her lap, palm up, and tell me a pack of lies. I was too in love to leave anything to chance. I wanted my destiny spelled out for me. I wanted Ruby to come to her senses. She did, after three men in the park raped her one night. She called me collect from the pay phone in the emergency room at Beth Israel. She was ready to try it another way.

She moved back in with her mother in Queens. Six weeks later, she showed up on East Twelfth Street, doubtful-seeming, though her veins were clean.

If Ruby could find a way to keep off smack for good, there wouldn't be cracks in my world, where vermin like Manny could wriggle in when I'm blind on bourbon, crying for myself. It's not that I kick Ruby out when she's shooting up, it's that she stops coming around. So I plug up the holes with whomever I can find. But now I have this dilemma: I want Ruby back in my bed. Nothing compares to her.

The first night Ruby and I made love, it was the height of summer. Salsa music blaring from some Puerto Rican's boom box clashed with the tin calliope sounds of an ice cream truck parked under my open window. But in my double bed at the back of the flat, the intrusions of the neighborhood faded. It was finally just Ruby and me—both of us sober.

When I saw her naked for the first time, I felt elation, the way an exulting mother must feel as her eyes first take in the body of her newborn, that unshakable faith in the existence of God. That's what it felt like to see Ruby without her clothes on. How else can one's mind account for something so perfect, so entrancing, so long-desired? Her firm, upturned breasts with their tiny eager nipples. Her narrow waist, slim hips. The dot of her navel and the swirl of black hair that hinted at the mystery hiding under it all—at first, it made touching her a little daunting. But she lay down next to me and fervently wanted to kiss. The force of passion coming from her slender body made the rest of it easy. I didn't worry about how to please her; I knew intuitively what her body wanted. I could smell it coming off her.

Her nipple stiffening in my mouth needed more pressure. I twisted it lightly with my fingers instead. Tugging it, rolling it, pulling it insistently, while my mouth returned to her kisses. She moaned and her long legs parted. That's how simple it was.

I knew she would be wet between her legs. My fingers slid into her snug pussy, and her whole body responded. An invisible wave of arousal rolled over her that I could feel in the pressure of her kiss. The muscular walls of her slick hole clamped around my two probing fingers, hugging them tightly, making it too plain that the thick, intrusive pricks of the pigs who'd raped her could only have succeeded in finding a way into her through sheer masculine determination. I knew how she had suffered.

Struggling, succumbing, three times successively. It was hard to believe her body had withstood the repeated violation. I shoved the pictures from my head. I centered my thoughts instead on the rhythm of her mound, how it urged my fingers to push in deeper. They did. Feeling my way, my fingers found the spot inside her that opened her completely, causing her thighs to spread wider, then she held herself spread, bearing down on my fingers as her slippery hole swelled around them.

I kissed my way down her ribs, down the flat expanse of her belly. Following the wispy trail of hairs that led to the world between her legs. I wanted my mouth all over her down there. It was what I had dreamed of, ached for. At last, she was offering it to me, wide open and engorged.

Sometimes I think about how easy it was to make her come. Two fingers up her hole and my tongue on her clit, then the river of shooting sparks gushed through her. And because I loved her it made me happy to make her come, even though afterward we lay together entwined with nothing left to talk about. Ruby and I were always silent when we finished making love. With those wealthy tricks uptown, it's more complicated. They need to discuss each detail. They practically draw you a map: the tit clamps here, the enema bag there, the length of rope tied like this, the gag last. The timing must be meticulous, the monologue rehearsed.

And with an uptight, paranoid guy like Manny it's even worse. There is no plan, no map, no discernible guideposts. Each gesture, each word is a toss of the dice: Will it lead to a kiss, or a bruised lip? I try not to lose sleep over it. If worse comes to worst, when Ruby arrives we'll shove the heavy bureau in front of the locked door. We'll go to my bed in the back of the flat, strip out of our clothes, and make love. Then I'll call the cops on Manny at last, when he's shouting obscenities out in the hall and slamming uselessly against the barricade.

Surrender Dorothy

Lisa Archer

Dorothy was my best friend in college. When we first met, she was, by her own definition, "straight." But her definition of straight changed like the wind. Dorothy was the first woman I had sex with, and vice versa. She framed this event as an act of charity—to help me determine whether I enjoyed having sex with women—as if she somehow represented all women on the planet. After having sex with me, she decided that she also had to sleep with her best friend from high school, who would be crushed if she ever found out that Dorothy had slept with any woman other than her. Thus one charitable act led to another, and soon Dorothy was shepherding me into sexual configurations of various numbers and genders. Since I was the shy one, I was happy to rely on her to organize our sexual forays. Until she finally came out as bisexual, she had a way of organizing group sex, then fleeing the scene, wracked with guilt. As I later discovered, Dorothy fantasized about having sex with virtually everyone she knew, and my burgeoning bisexuality provided an opportunity for her to test-drive some encounters that would otherwise have been difficult to rationalize, given that she still called herself "straight."

My first threesome was orchestrated by Dorothy and a guy she was fucking named Matt, who happened to be my ex-boyfriend's roommate. What I remember most about the experience was Matt's effort to make sure everyone felt included by mentioning both our names as he came: "Oh Dorothy... oh Lisa." As I fell asleep that night, I couldn't help feeling as if I'd just had my first bisexual experience, even though I'd already identified as bisexual for a year and had sex with both men and women individually. Nonetheless, if I had sex with a man at 7 P.M., and a woman at 8, who's to say I didn't go through a heterosexual phase at 7 and find my true lesbian identity an hour later? After my first ménage à trois, I felt as if I'd jumped through the final hoop of true bisexual identity.

We finally cornered Dorothy into coming out as bisexual. It was a bit like gang warfare, and it happened during a surprise party that I organized for her nineteenth birthday.

Several months earlier, Dorothy had confided her core childhood masturbation fantasy in the wee hours of the morning, when our inhibitions were down. Since the age of seven, she had fantasized about crawling through a paddy wagon of authority figures, consisting of her grammar school teachers, camp counselors, and babysitters. Eventually, she came to the last link in the chain—the school principal, who would spank her hardest of all. That was the part of the fantasy that made her come.

I admired Dorothy's sexual precocity. But I also realized that she was telling her childhood fantasy from the perspective of her present eighteen-year-old self. She was thus embellishing this particular fantasy with a knowledge of sexuality that she couldn't possibly have had as a seven-year-old. I concluded that the paddy wagon was a present fantasy, which Dorothy was unconsciously projecting onto her childhood— probably because she felt less guilty telling it in the past tense.

In any case, spanking was Dorothy's biggest turn-on. She wanted to be punished. Unfortunately, she had a hard time asking her sex partners to whack her on the butt. After all, we were only eighteen, and most of us hadn't evolved much in the way of sexual communication skills. Organizing group sex, then fleeing the scene, was a circuitous and ultimately unsatisfying route to getting what she wanted. I decided to make it easier for her by giving her a surprise paddy wagon for her birthday.

I got stuck on the question of which authority figures to invite. We were in college at the time, but professors were out of the question. Graduate students, on the other hand, were predatory beasts, lying in wait to seduce young undergrads, hoping to gain some semblance of respect, which the university denied them.

So I invited Megan, my neurotic girlfriend, who just last week had been studying for her Ph.D. exams while Dorothy, Matt, and I fucked in my bedroom several blocks away. Megan would have been happier if I had forewarned her of the threesome, or even asked her permission. But at the time I was unpracticed in the ways of polyamory, which is a nice way of saying I was cheating. I also invited Megan's best friend, Michael, who was Dorothy's former teaching assistant. Megan and Michael had slept together, I knew, but Michael was primarily attracted to men. His boyfriend, Daniel, was an undergraduate and a mutual friend of Dorothy's and mine. (Dorothy had engineered a threesome with Daniel and Michael the summer before.) So I invited Daniel too. I also invited Chelsea, my quiet bisexual roommate, and her loud boyfriend Jeff, a graduate student in the French Department, who wanted to be bisexual for political reasons. Martin was Jeff's best friend and a local drunk. He was capable of brilliant conversation and occasionally fucked my girlfriend, but was otherwise generally useless. Jeff and Martin were thirty and thirty-two years old, which seemed ancient to me at eighteen, so I thought they'd make good authority figures for the paddy wagon. Finally I invited my ex-boyfriend Tom, who could be a stick in the mud. Dorothy didn't really like him, but since I was inviting Matt, and Tom was Matt's roommate, I had to invite Tom too.

I told all the guests about the paddy wagon, although I didn't tell them it was Dorothy's masturbation fantasy. I just told them she'd like it a lot. I was secretly hoping the event would turn into an orgy—although I didn't tell everyone that, either. To decrease the likelihood that people would stomp off in disgust, I tried to invite bisexuals, or at least people who were willing to have sex with both men and women.

The night of the surprise party, I invited Dorothy and Matt to come over at around 8, just to hang out and celebrate her birthday, perhaps with another threesome. The guests arrived an hour early. They were supposed to stay in the living room, so Dorothy wouldn't see them when she first walked in. When the doorbell rang, they quickly got into paddy wagon formation—standing in line with their legs spread so that Dorothy could crawl through. I opened the door for Dorothy and Matt. We chatted in the kitchen for a few minutes. Then I quickly led them into the living room, so that the guests wouldn't get leg cramps from holding their paddy wagon positions too long.

"Surprise!" they yelled, as I opened the door.

Dorothy's jaw dropped. "Oh my God, what are you all doing?"

"You have to crawl through our legs!" shouted Jeff, who was at the front of the line.

It took a few seconds for Dorothy to get it. Then she blushed deep red and ran out of the room.

"Hey, wait!" Matt and I grabbed her arms and dragged her back in, virtually kicking and screaming.

"Come on! Crawl through!" the guests demanded. "We can't stand here all day, you know." They were starting to fidget.

"No," Dorothy insisted. "Not unless everyone else does."

"You first. It's your birthday."

Dorothy blushed deeper, but finally got on her hands and knees in front of the line. She hesitated. Matt and I stood right behind her in case she tried to bolt.

She looked back at us. "I can't believe you're making me do this," she said.

Dorothy started to crawl. As soon as she was halfway through Jeff's legs, he administered a loud whack on the butt, then drummed on her ass with both hands.

"Ouch!" she wailed. "Ow, ow, ow." I'd positioned Jeff at the front of the line, because I knew he would spank hard and boldly—demonstrating to everyone else how it was supposed to be done. Chelsea came after Jeff. Her spanking was tentative, but Megan's was hard and stingy—she was a mean hardass, when it came right down to it.

Michael was next in line. To everyone's surprise and delight, he grabbed the elastic waistband of Dorothy's sweatpants and pulled them down, exposing her bare butt.

"Oooooh," we cooed.

"Hold on. That's not fair," Dorothy protested. But Michael and Matt were already caressing her naked ass.

"You don't want us to stop now, do you?" Michael asked, as he spanked her ass with one hand, stroking it with the other.

Dorothy didn't say anything. But she was sighing and wiggling her butt, clearly enjoying it. I could see Matt's cock swelling under the zipper of his jeans. He knelt down beside her, and they kissed. Dorothy was still on all fours between Michael's legs. Michael was still spanking her, and there were three people left in the paddy wagon line: Michael's boyfriend, Daniel; my ex-boyfriend Tom; and Martin, the drunk.

Then mayhem broke loose. Daniel spanked Michael, Megan spanked me, as about five hands stroked and spanked Dorothy's butt. Michael slipped his fingers between

Dorothy's wet pussy lips. Dorothy was squirming. Matt unzipped his pants.

"Hold on," Dorothy interrupted, standing up. "I'm not fucking all of you!" Michael, Matt, and I exchanged glances.

"Oh yes, you are!" we said in unison.

Matt and I grabbed her and held her still on all fours.

Dorothy screamed, but there was no one to save her. My next-door neighbor was deaf, and the people upstairs were insane. They were building a bomb shelter on the second floor. Screams were nothing out of the ordinary.

Michael took off his pants. Daniel stood behind him, grinding his crotch against Michael's butt. "Why don't you fuck her while I fuck you?"

"Hold on there. Ladies first." Megan sat down beside Michael, wearing a strap-on, which she must have grabbed from my bedroom when she saw where all this was going. Meanwhile, Dorothy had stopped screaming. Matt put several fingers inside her, as I caressed her butt.

"You OK?" I asked.

"I guess so. For the moment." Still on her hands and knees, she wiggled her ass in the air.

"She's really wet," said Matt. I stroked her clit. She was dripping. I moved my fingers back and forth, then in circles. She moaned and squirmed.

Megan was wearing a huge red dildo. She covered it in lube and pressed the tip against Dorothy's cunt. When it was all the way in, Megan waited as Dorothy adjusted to the huge dildo.

Meanwhile Michael and Daniel had positioned themselves in front of Dorothy. Daniel stroked his cock right in front of Dorothy's face. When he was really hard, he put a condom and lube on his cock. Michael got down on all fours, and Daniel entered him from behind. Dorothy, Megan, and I all got excited, because we love watching gay porn; it was an even bigger turn-on live.

Megan pumped the big red dildo in and out of Dorothy's cunt.

"Harder!" Dorothy demanded. The live gay porn had apparently transformed her from a quasi-resistant gangbang victim into an insatiable slut. As Megan thrust harder, Daniel did too, and for the next fifteen minutes, the loudest sounds in the room were those of pelvises slapping against butts. Matt and I stood by, administering random whacks to Dorothy's ass. Chelsea, Jeff, Martin, and Tom had retreated to the sidelines and were providing a running pseudo-intellectual commentary, which I could barely hear over everyone's groans.

Just as I noticed Matt had a condom on his cock, he threw me down on my back. I'd gotten so absorbed in spanking Dorothy that I hadn't even realized how wet I was. Dorothy looked up as Matt entered me, and I recognized that furtive gleam in her eyes. I dragged myself closer to her, as Matt lay on top of me thrusting. Dorothy leaned over and licked my nipples. At that point, my ex-boyfriend Tom stomped off, slamming the door loudly. I didn't know how he and Matt were going to live together after this, but at that moment, I didn't care, and I don't think anyone else did either. Meanwhile, Chelsea, Jeff, and Martin the drunk retreated to my bedroom to have comparatively boring sex with each other.

After an hour of hardcore fucking and multiple orgasms, we collapsed, exhausted. As we were lying around in a sweaty, pulsating heap, Michael asked, "So Dorothy, does this mean you're finally a card-carrying bisexual?"

"I guess I'm not in Kansas anymore," she sighed. A big satiated grin spread across her face.

Party of One

Elise Tanner

You tell me to dress up, to wear something sexy; we're going to the most expensive restaurant in town. I guess Villa du Monde, but you've picked Botticelli's, surprising me—and yes, I discover, it's even more expensive than the Villa. Luckily, I've picked my only dress, the sea-blue one with the long slit in the front that comes up almost to midthigh and plunges in back, leaving my woman's symbol tattoo for all the snooty patrons to gawk at. You're wearing your tux, which makes them gawk even more. But no one has the guts to say anything: you have that no-nonsense look about you, after all.

The food and wine are incredible; I'm just starting my third glass of Merlot when you tell me I might not want to drink quite so much.

Why's that? I ask you.

Silently, smiling, you pass me a small gift box, wrapped in gold. I open it and stare in surprise at the black leather blindfold. I glancd around, nervous that the rich patrons will notice my face turning bright red, that somehow they will realize the bolt of energy that's surging through my body, flooding my pussy in an instant. You're still smiling.

It's beautiful, I whisper, hoarse....

"Remember you once told me your favorite fantasy was to be led into a hotel room blindfolded, where someone was waiting to fuck you? And you would never find out who that person was?"

I can feel my nipples stiffening, braless under the slinky dress. I cross my legs uncomfortably, and nod.

"Is that still your favorite fantasy?"

Yes, I say, knowing now what is about to happen—or thinking I do.

"When we finish our meal, there will be a limousine waiting out front to take us to the Beaumont. Do you understand?"

My stomach does flip-flops. My head spins. I nod slowly, hardly able to breathe.

"Tell me now if there are any limits you have, other than the ones you discussed in that fantasy."

I look at you blankly, seeing right through your body to the stripped-down, raw essence of your soul: the lover of control, the giver of adventure. And I know, in that instant, that there is absolutely nothing you could ask me to do that I wouldn't.

Nothing, I tell you. *Nothing at all.*

You lift your glass, toast me.

"To danger," you say, and I feel the throbbing between my thighs.

• • •

Limousines? The Beaumont? Botticelli's? I know it's a big birthday, maybe the biggest, but how are you affording all this? You're a college professor, for God's sake, and a women's studies professor at that. I have a fantasy for an instant that my stone butch girlfriend is only masquerading as a professor, that you're really a gangster, kissing me goodbye in the morning and driving off to "class" only to go kill a bunch of people or deliver drugs or something. But, that aside, I know you must have been saving for this night forever. And I've long since learned not to resist your shows of affection, but just to accept them, with all the abandon and apprehension with which I accept my mother's love. Only yours is a thousand times more real.

• • •

In the back of the limo, you kiss me, hard, your tongue driving into me with an attitude of utter possession. I feel your hands on my breasts, pinching my hard nipples through the silk dress; I feel them sliding up my thighs and stroking my juicing pussy, at first through the thong and then underneath. I moan, about to come, but you know better than to give me that sort of relief before an adventure like this. Instead, you tell me to take off my underwear, and I do, and you tuck it into the pocket of your tux.

"You're ready, now," you tell me.

"Ready for anything," I say, and I am.

• • •

When the driver lets us out at the curb, you tip him twenty dollars and tell him we'll be here for several hours. "It may take all night," you tell him, and my knees go weak. "We'll call you."

In the lobby, you take my hand and press a plastic key card into it.

"Room 1519," you tell me. "Put the blindfold on before you enter the room, and take off your dress, shoes, and stockings as soon as you're inside. You take two-foot, ten-inch steps, so the bed is four steps straight ahead and two steps to the left. Get into it."

"Aren't you...?"

You shake your head. "This is anonymous, remember? It's all yours. The person in the hotel room will not speak under any circumstances, but if you wish to stop the scene, just say my name and it will stop immediately."

I kiss you on the cheek, afraid, abandoned, but somehow intensely aroused. Who will be waiting for me? A demanding dyke with a strap-on, like you? A dedicated sadist with nipple clamps for my tits and a big paddle for my ass? A perfumed femme in a slinky dress like mine? A young stripper with a shaved pussy, a student who whores on the side?

I take the elevator up with an obviously wealthy older couple; I fantasize that they know exactly what I'm doing, heading to an illicit, anonymous lesbian tryst on the top floor. It makes my pussy even wetter. Thank God they get off on the fourteenth floor; I wasn't looking forward to putting on the blindfold in the hall with them watching.

I step off the elevator, find the room. I still have the gift box with me. I open it up and take out the leather blindfold.

For an instant, I listen at the door. I can't hear anything; the soundproofing is flawless.

I glance up and down the hall and see no one. Quickly, I put on the blindfold and insert the key card into the lock.

The door beeps softly on the first try, and I push the door open and go in.

It's the smell that hits me first, unfamiliar yet comforting. I don't know what's unfamiliar about it, but it's human, rich, and thick—like you when you're sweaty after a long night of fucking me.

I close the door and remember your instructions. I shrug off the long dress, not even caring that I let it crumple to the floor. I'll get it dry cleaned later. I kick off my shoes, then take off my stockings, breathing that familiar yet unfamiliar smell.

Now naked, I move into the room.

Four steps forward, two steps left. I feel the edge of the

bed. I hear classical music, playing softly from a good stereo. It's one of Chopin's *Nocturnes,* and I'm sure you'd know which one from two or three notes. Underneath it, I hear rhythmic breathing, but no words.

I feel my way along the edge of the bed. There's a starched corner pulled back, open for me. Obeying your final command, I climb into bed to meet my lover.

When flesh hits flesh, I feel it, instinctively, but I don't put it together for an instant. The strong, thick arms curving around me. The muscular legs entwining with mine. The great weight on top of me, the unfamiliar scent becoming suddenly familiar, then unfamiliar again. The scratch of whiskers against my face as he kisses me, the pressure around my wrists as he takes them and holds them against the bed, the hard cock pressing insistently against my thigh. The surge of terror in my belly as I realize what you've done, the sudden feeling of being at risk of being violated, at risk of being hurt.

Then, as I feel his tongue against mine, I flash on the million times I've had this fantasy—an anonymous man in a hotel room—and my whole body surges with sudden excitement, my flesh electric everywhere he touches me. It's been a long, long time with only my fantasies, and somehow you knew that this fantasy of the hotel that I confessed to you had been edited slightly to change the gender of the other participant. How could you have known that? But you did, and that's why I love you, and that's one of the two reasons I relax into the anonymous man's body and let him kiss me. I let his tongue ravish me, let his cock strain against my belly as he climbs on top of me and holds me against the bed. The other reason is that I want this, and I've wanted this forever. Not to have sex with a man, but to be utterly, completely overwhelmed by my desires, more importantly overwhelmed by *you.* To have you push me beyond my resistance, beyond my fears, beyond my restrictions, to give in to my uncomfortable desires, to feel this cock against my belly and know that it's going inside me. To feel my pussy juicing as the weight of a naked, unknown body holds me to the bed.

He kisses my neck, then my ear, eliciting soft moans from my lips. His breath is hot against my flesh. He gently turns my head so that he can bite the back of my neck, making me squirm underneath him. Then he releases my wrists and moves down, his tongue tracing a path from my neck to shoulders to upturned armpits, then down to my breasts. I feel his hot mouth around my nipple, feel it growing even harder between his teeth. He lingers just long enough to make me squirm and shiver and moan, and then his tongue draws a figure eight over my belly, and I realize with a rush where he's headed. He gently parts my legs as his face settles between my thighs, as his tongue finds its place in my cleft, pressing against my swollen, throbbing clit and licking down to taste the juices of my flooding cunt. God, he's good—not as good as you, perhaps, but incredible enough to make me think I'm going to come right away, then to sense it and back off so that I can suffer in divine torment while he teases me. He holds me there on the edge, teasing my clit with his tongue-tip, his hands parting my lips and exposing my entrance. Two fingers inside me, smoothly, gently penetrating, then pressing firmly up against my G-spot, make me do it—make me come, hard, harder than I expected, and my ass rises high off the bed as the surges go through my naked body.

Even I'm surprised at what happens next. I say, "Turn around. Get on top of me. I want to suck your dick."

He doesn't speak, just like you said. I haven't sucked cock in so many years, I'm sure I'm not very good at it, but I'm so hungry for him I don't care. This is about my pleasure, and when he settles his hard body down on top of me, top to tail, I realize he is just a little shorter than average, which puts his cock in exactly the right position as his mouth descends on my sex again. I take it in my hand, for a split second not sure what to do with it, and then my hunger overtakes me and I start sucking, gulping it desperately, rubbing it all over my face and feeling the smooth hardness as I smell him up close. I tongue his balls while his tongue wriggles its way between my lips again and he begins licking my clit—upside down this time, which is all that saves me from screaming that I'm too sensitive. You must have told him everything about me, because one spit-lubed thumb gently works its way between my ass cheeks, stroking my tight hole, and I only have to coax him a little before he slips it in and goes back to licking my clit. God, I want to make him come, in my mouth or all over my tits, but if I have to wait another instant to feel him inside me I'm going to go mad. I whisper, "Fuck me, fuck me from behind," and he obediently relinquishes his grip on my pussy and rolls me over onto my hands and knees. He's so well trained—where did you *get* this guy?—that he tucks not two but three pillows under my belly to hold me up while he moves behind me. He positions himself, his cock finding my pussy. I moan as he slowly pushes in, and his hand reaches under me and finds my clit before I even have time to reach for it.

He seems to know right away that he can make me come in that position, but he holds off, teasing me, reading my body as if he's had a college course in it, which he probably has. He toys with me, his cock sliding into me rhythmically while I get closer and closer, hovering on the edge until he forces me to cool off so that he can fuck me some more.

I feel his thumb on my ass again, and I am barely coherent enough to gasp, "There too, there too," so when I feel his thumb pressing against my asshole all I can do is shake my head and say, "No, no, no," until he gets the idea. I feel the cold drop of lube between my cheeks, massaged in by his thumb. He pulls out of my pussy and slides his cock between my ass-cheeks—the first cock I've ever felt there, except yours.

He enters me slowly, hearing me gasp and moaning, "Wait...wait...wait...OK, now, now," before pushing in smoothly and penetrating my anus. I'm moaning louder than ever, and as he fucks my ass he doesn't forget about my clit; his rhythm is perfect, his fingers matching the long strokes as he brings me to the edge of orgasm.

But before I come, I pause, because absorbed as I am, as full of the smell of him that I am, I can't ignore the new scent, one so familiar I almost don't notice it. Then I hear the breathing, off to the side, as if you're sitting in a chair near the bed, watching us—and I know, all of a sudden, that this moment wasn't just for me; it was for both of us.

Then I come, harder than I've ever come without you fisting me, and my muscles clench and spasm around my phantom lover as I reach out for you, grab your hand, and come again.

• • •

Walking unsteadily into the bright morning, my expensive dress rumpled, I see you drinking your coffee in the lobby and I head for you. I take the seat next to yours, because I can't bend down to kiss you without losing control of my knees. I curl up in the easy chair and you kiss me.

"The limousine driver's long gone, so we'll have to take a cab home, I'm afraid. Pricey."

"We could take the bus."

You chuckle. "Did you have a nice night in your hotel room?"

"It was the best birthday ever," I tell you. "Mostly because of who was watching me."

"Whatever do you mean?"

"Never mind," I say. "I'll be remembering this birthday for a long, long time."

"As will I," you tell me, and offer me a drink of your coffee. I savor it: cream, no sugar, just like you.

What She's Worth

Michelle Scalise

I study her eyes, sapphire blue and clear as the sea. Unlike her husband, she's more angry than scared, and I like that. She surveys the room, searching for a way out or a weapon. The stack of woman's magazines I dug out of the trash at Penn Station rest in my lap. I like to mix up the fonts, so that they'll resemble the ransom notes in movies. The red light overhead hemorrhages on every image, staining the model's phony smiles.

With a pair of scissors in my hand, I wave them in her direction and say, "I'll bet you read shit like this." Flipping through the pages of perfumed ads, I find the table of contents: "How to Flirt Like a Pro," "Sexual Techniques to Keep Him Satisfied." Ripping the glossy cover from the spine, I fling it at the woman tied and gagged in my living room. "All Dean needs is some head, Karen. And hell, it's not like he takes very long to come."

She's glaring now. Her voice fights beneath the silver duct tape stretched across her lips.

Two floors below, sirens scream through crowded streets as night slinks between the buildings. I grab the stereo remote and turn up the music. Kurt Cobain is begging to be raped. Karen struggles to turn a bit, gazing down at the traffic. Short dark curls, framing her heart-shaped face, flick across her cheekbones like a slash. Crimson bleeds on her skin, running down her long legs like snakes. She is a mix of designer labels, from the small gold chain at her throat to the tennis shoes on her feet.

"But you gotta swallow," I continue. "None of that spitting-in-a-tissue when he's finished."

I'm doing a half-assed job of pasting individual letters onto a piece of notebook paper and laughing because she looks as if, given the chance, she'd gladly put a bullet in my head.

I grab her wallet from the small purse she carried. "Fifty-three dollars?" I say, tossing the cash onto the sofa. "Christ, I could get more mugging a Girl Scout!" She's trying to speak again, but I ignore her and pull out a black-and-white photo, the kind you pose for in a closet-size booth. Karen is smiling bright as sunshine in the picture, both her arms wrapped around a pinched-faced woman. I flip the photograph over and read aloud, " 'Me and Brandi.' Are you fucking her? Because, nothing personal, but you could do better."

Karen shakes her head, her muffled voice grumbling.

I pull the switchblade from my black Doc Martens, nearing her side as I flick it through the air like a swashbuckler. She gives a gratifying yelp when I yank a corner of the tape from her mouth. "I'm sorry, Karen, I didn't get that. Was there something you wanted to share?"

"She's just a friend, you lunatic!" she yells.

I thrust the blade at her pale throat, then gently scrape a trickle of sweat. Her breasts, small and hard, cling to the white T-shirt she wears. "You're really going to have to lower your voice, sweetheart," I say, brushing the hair from her face. "Sorry, about the heat. My air conditioner went on the fritz yesterday."

"How do you know my husband?" she asks, the disdain barely concealed. "Have you been following me?"

"I don't stalk," I say. "Where's the surprise in that? I just scope the parking lots of private gyms and tennis courts where people like you hang out, looking for the right girl...or guy. When you showed up to work out, I jimmied the lock on your BMW and waited in the back seat. I love the smell of leather. I had a boyfriend once who could only fuck in cars. I'd climb right into his lap while he drove through rush hour traffic— never got in an accident, either."

"Do you know Dean?" she asks. "Are you having an affair with him? Because, if you are, I don't care. You're welcome to him. Just let me go."

"Thanks for the offer of your Ken doll, but I think I'll pass." I nudge her chin with the blade, retaping her into silence. "I've got to mail the ransom note. And then we'll see how much you're worth to him. Don't make a sound while I'm gone." Reaching down, I rub my thumb against her nipple till I can see its hard outline beneath the cotton. I want to suck it into my mouth until she moans, but I like to drag out the game as long as I can bear it. Anticipation is a wet dream. "Good girl," I say. The red light can't hide the blush of her cheeks.

I close the door behind me, humming as I head down to the trash chute at the end of the hall.

When I return, I find Karen tipping the chair back and forth, like a broken rocking horse, as she attempts to move across the floor. Laughing, I pull her back to the open window. "You've destroyed my faith in you, sweetie." Slipping my knife tenderly under her shirt, I slice up through the material until it hangs from her shoulders.

Finally, she looks scared.

"You want to know how I'm acquainted with your husband?" I circle her, licking at her ear. Her perfume is a musk, but she wears it lightly. A breeze, accenting the heat, flutters through the room, waving the black curtains out like a parachute. "I gave him a blowjob he'll never forget right here in this chair." I've got her from behind, her breasts cupped in my hands. I hear her breath, harsh and fast, as I massage her nipples. "I had him between my lips." She shakes her head.

"And if you're good, Karen," I whisper, "I may let you go."

I get wet just saying the words.

From a bookshelf in the corner, nestled behind my collection of Victorian erotica, I pull out the dildo I've been envisioning up her cunt since I first saw her. The music, slow and achingly sad, wails as I spin and sway. I feel the red light searing into me like a brand. Lifting my arms, I remove the tiny black dress I'm wearing. I keep the boots on.

In her white exercise outfit, drenched in scarlet and shadows, she looks like an orchid in a hothouse.

I kneel at her side, cutting away at her shorts until I can pull them to her ankles.

Karen groans when I grab a nipple between my teeth, pulling and licking till I feel her arch into me. Coiling my fingers into her hair, I force her still. "I want you to see the way I sucked him off." Sliding the dildo in and out between my lips, I mesmerize her. She's forgotten about Dean, or else she enjoys picturing her husband in my mouth. I almost wish I'd brought him along so that I might take turns on them.

Drawing the cock out, I twine it down between my legs, stroking my clit. I'm inches from her face when I shove it into my cunt. "Do you like watching me ride him, Karen?" She doesn't make a sound, but she doesn't look away either. My heart's pounding so fast that I almost lose track of where I'm at in the game. I pull out when I feel myself ready to come.

Leaning down, I rip at the tape, ready to tear through rock just to get to her mouth. "Open wide. I want you to taste how hard I fucked your husband." She accepts half the dildo in one swallow. I start her off easy, grinding slow at first, until she's used to the pressure at the back of her throat. The look of lust in her eyes is like a storm swirling. I push deeper and she takes it in. "You're doing good, sweetie. Lick my juice off him." Her tongue, slick and pink, runs along its shaft, circling the tip.

I get lightheaded watching her. She groans, and I want to grab the back of her neck and force her down on me until she drowns in my cunt, but I know I can't take the chance of untying her yet.

As I straddle her lap, she turns to meet my kiss. The dildo slides into her easily. "You wanna fuck him with me?" She's rising up to reach each thrust, controlling the speed of the fuck. The friction of the cock, with her warm cunt rubbing against me, drives any thoughts of her husband out of my mind. I squeeze one of her breasts, letting the nipple, red and hard, glide into my mouth.

I press further, her body growing tense beneath my touch, until I can feel the scream building. Suddenly her orgasm is raging through me. Pounding the dildo in as far as I can reach, I come all over her cunt.

After I've had a minute of licking the sweat from her skin, I gather up her belongings and slip my dress over her head. "It's a little small, but we can't have you driving home naked."

"You did all this just to fuck me?" she asks. "I don't under-stand."

I get her feet untied. "Yes, you do. You've never come that good in your life. Uptight yuppies like you and Dean, with your white-bread sex lives, always have nasty fantasies. I've never found one yet I couldn't play the game with."

I free her hands and she massages her ankles, then stands. "So you kidnapped Dean too."

"I found your photo in his wallet," I say. Straightening the sheer sleeves at her wrist, I give her a short kiss. "Figured the two of you probably belonged to the same gym." I lead her to the door. "Time to go, sweetie. Your husband will be expecting you home."

Digging through her bag, she comes up with a pale blue business card. "I'll be working late next week." She smiles, then quickly looks away. "I park in the east-end garage, second level."

"Sorry, Karen." I admire the way she purses her lips. I kiss her again, and the touch of her tongue snakes into my cunt. "Half the fun is in the element of surprise," I explain, knowing that I'll be waiting for her again in the dark.

Hands

Ariel Hart

It's all about hands, you see. Everything. Life. Lust. Hands do the work. Hands give love, punishment, joy, cruelty. Hands commit acts of shame. Hands make the money. And because of this, hands are very important. Hands have to look good. And that's where I come in.

I keep moving. I always keep moving. That's my secret. But since I've told you, it isn't a secret anymore, is it? People tell me their secrets all the time. Maybe it comes from being poked and stroked. Maybe it comes from being touched in a way that no one else touches them and from being made beautiful. At least until the cuticles grow in or the linen tips wear off. My customers tell me their dreams, their desires, their disappointments, their frustrations. And they feel good afterward. They feel good for many reasons.

I've been told that I have very understanding eyes, dark and full of compassion. I've been told a lot of things. Maybe people think I don't understand, because I speak with an accent: I am not from around here. Maybe that's why they talk so much and so honestly. But I understand every word.

I come from a place where there is more poverty and sadness than in this place. Where people worry about their families going hungry instead of broken nails. But broken nails and broken hearts are my salvation.

I can see it happening the moment they sit in my chair. They relax, unwind, unravel. If I am working in a posh salon, we might be in a small, comfortable private room and they might be wearing a silky robe embroidered with the salon's name. This makes it easier. Easier to see. Easier to reach. They talk and talk. I listen. With my ears and with my eyes.

I deftly use my little curved scissors, clippers, and knives. I file away at imperfections and replace them with smoothness. At some point, I realize that pieces of my clients are chipping away, falling free, being liberated. By the time I squeeze droplets of astringent onto their fingertips, they are lost. Sometimes there is a little sigh of pleasure, of relief. Sometimes it only shows in their faces. And that's when I set to work.

I place their hands together, as if in prayer, then surround them with a steaming washcloth. Then I open them toward me and release a dollop of pink cream into the heel of each palm and work it into the skin. My touch is sure and firm yet gentle. I work on the palm first, then extend the massage to include each finger. I knead and pull. Occasionally they say something like "This is my favorite part," but when they do, their voice is weak and far off and their eyes are murky. I can tell that they are moist between the legs or that they are hard, depending on their sex. This is the moment I suggest something extra, something more: a deep penetrating body massage, a waxing, a special cleansing treatment.

I once had a regular customer, an attractive, well-coiffed woman in her late forties, who at this point liked me to touch her from the other side of the table. Mrs. Winston's legs would be slightly spread. Her satiny robe would be pushed up past her knees, and she would wear nothing underneath. I would reach forward and insert my thumb into her cunt so that my other fingers would be free to stroke her clitoris, which would already be swollen and erect. Her thighs would be soaked. The seat of her robe would be damp.

Sometimes, I wouldn't even have to move my hand. Mrs. Winston would press her hips in tiny circles against my palm. When I looked into her face, her eyes would be closed and her jaw would be slack. The contraction of her cunt muscles would draw my thumb in even further. There would be a hundred little heartbeats in her pussy, which would start off strong, then ebb like a disoriented tide. When the pulsations stopped, she and I would proceed just as before. We would never speak of what happened. But at the end of my shift, there would always be a sealed envelope waiting out in the reception area, my name written in sharp, frilly script. And inside the envelope would be a generous tip.

Mrs. Winston was a steady customer. She made an appointment each week without fail, sometimes two. Her hands were in good shape. She washed no dishes; she did no housework. Yet she seemed to need her weekly treatments. Once, I did something different. Instead of using my hand, I applied my mouth. I just fell to my knees and crushed my face between her legs. She gasped in disbelief yet she didn't push me away. I pursed my lips around her fiery little clitoris and sucked. I sucked it into my mouth and trapped it against my teeth. She came even faster than usual, but she did not return to the salon. However, at the end of my shift, in a sealed envelope, there was a gratuity even larger than the one she generally gave. That was the last I saw of her.

Another time, there was a client who wanted a depilatory, a shave. The salon was busy, so they asked me to do it. We had a special table for this in a different room. The woman was young and slender with short, spiked hair that was peroxided the color of straw. I later heard talk that she was a powerful person in the music industry, but I never learned what she did.

When I entered the room, she was waiting, sitting on the high, cushioned cot, smoking a cigarette. "I'd like the whole works," she told me. Meaning, she wanted to be shaved from her ankles to her belly. First, I had her lie back. I lifted her salon gown and had her spread her legs. There was a tuft of jet-black hair so thick I couldn't even see her pussy lips through it. I grabbed a pair of scissors and, with a comb, began pulling her pubic hairs away from her skin, then snipping away the clumps of fuzz. Slowly, a fleshy mound began to emerge. Her labia was full, like a mouth about to pout.

"You have wonderful hands," she said shyly as I slid the comb above her narrow slit. I noticed that the hairs were soaking wet around her hole. The aroma was nice: of sex and sweat and the sea. I gave her a close trim, then began to wipe the clippings away with a hot, wet towel. I worked the towel between the chinks of her cunt and swabbed both sets of lips. Her knees eased wider and wider apart. I sensed what she wanted, but it was too soon and she was a brand-new customer. So, I reached for the shaving cream, which was kept piping hot in a dispenser.

I began with her legs, slathering the heated cream along the entire length. I opened a fresh razor and moved it from ankle-bone to knee, leaving behind slick, smooth skin. Her cunt waited impatiently. A ribbon of its juice drooled down the crack of her ass and onto the cushion below. I noticed this when I tucked a soft, fluffy towel under her bottom.

It is very tricky shaving cunts, especially ones with such prominent lips. I applied swirls of the warm cream to her mons, then ran a finger down the chink in the center to expose her slit. There was a change in her breathing, especially when I cupped my hand over one half of her pussy, making sure to encase the lips to protect them from the razor's edge. I started at the bottom, then worked my way up, moving from thigh muscle to delicate, perfumed flesh. Then I did the other side. The dark hairs fell away. I cleaned the razor often in a bowl of steaming water, exposing the vulnerable white flesh hiding beneath her garden of fur.

The woman's clitoris stood free, proud, almost as though it wanted to be noticed. I positioned two fingers on either side of the fleshy button to shave the stray hairs surrounding its hood. She shuddered. I scraped the skin clean until it resembled a plump peach, though it was much softer than that pulpy fruit. From the faucet, I drew another pan of warm water. I dipped a small hand towel into it, then wrung it out. I wiped her legs clean of shaving cream, took another towel, wet it, then applied the damp heat to her cunt. She sighed, clasped her hand on top of mine, and held it there.

"I'm not finished," I said softly. I reached for the other dispenser filled with hot lotion. I rubbed it into my hands, then slathered it onto her legs. Firmly, I massaged her calves, the taut muscles behind her knees, her thighs. Then I squeezed out more molten cream. I worked it onto her mound, in between the flaps of her labia, with firm fingers. I took her clit between both thumbs and kneaded it like a tiny, fleshy bit of dough. "It's important to keep the sensitive skin moist," I told her. And she agreed with a nod.

She came.

I could see the clenching, the spasms of her orgasm. Whimpering and shaking, she grabbed the sides of the table. Her pussy lips fluttered and gulped. I wanted so much to kiss them—they seemed to be in need of a kiss. But after Mrs. Winston, I wasn't sure how she'd react. Finally, I kissed her cunt anyway. She tasted salty and sweet. I flicked her swollen clitoris gently with my tongue. Then I took each flower-like lip into my mouth, tugged it, and released it so that I could watch it unfurl.

She pulled on my hair. *Should I stop?* I wondered. *No.* She shook her head and motioned for me to move on top of her. I hesitated a moment, then slid my white pantyhose down to my shoes. I straddled her face, knowing I was very wet myself, hoping she wouldn't drown. What did she think of my plump, little morsel as I lowered it onto her face? I sensed that her tongue had been in places like this before. I allowed myself a pleasure I rarely do as I pressed my mouth into her crotch. I came, too. But somehow, it didn't feel right.

As I finished pulsing against her face, she climaxed again. Quickly and deeply, guiltily. I took another fresh washcloth to swab her cheeks and chin. Kira explained that she was from out of town and was only visiting her company's New York office for the day. "I thought I deserved a treat," she whispered as she stood on wobbly legs, crushed two twenties into my hand, then left, thanking me.

I don't want you to get the idea that I stalk customers who are lost and lonely, or that I'm a prostitute. It's nothing like that. But when I see people aroused or at ease, erect or wet, something inside of me gives way, gives in. I figure, why not? What have I got to lose? I live alone. I don't have many friends here, and there's no family. It makes me feel...something. It makes me feel as if I'm part of something.

Do the salons know? Do they care? Their main concern is that customers keep coming back. Is it illegal? Probably. But I don't stay in one place too long. That's why I try to keep moving. It's safer that way. I don't get too close. I don't get too attached. And I never get caught.

In the men's grooming parlors, it's different. Maybe because guys are slower to admit what they're feeling. I can count the incidents with men on the fingers of one hand. They aren't used to being touched, unless it's in a sexual way. Casual touching makes them uncomfortable. They don't know what to do when someone strokes their skin, pampers them. Women love this, live for this—men look as though they want to crawl under a rock, at first.

So, I try to get them to relax. To talk about themselves. It isn't easy but after a while they do. After a while, they like it. And that's the key: to help calm them. It makes me feel good, to see a guy walk into my room twisted into a big, tense knot and in a few moments have him puddling into my hand. It's an amazing transformation—and all because of a few well-placed rubs.

When the manicure is almost finished and I begin massaging his hands, the man usually becomes uneasy. I imagine this is because he feels good, too good, and he doesn't want to give in to it. Maybe he thinks it's a sign of weakness. But when I see him shifting around uncomfortably in his seat, that's when I set to work, kneading his palms, tugging on his creamy fingers as if I'm jerking him off. If he's wearing a robe, his arousal is evident by the pup tent in his lap. Otherwise, his trousers are uncomfortably tight, making the bulge of his stiff cock unmistakable.

The next moment is a highly sensitive one. But something, some silent signal from him, urges me either to continue or to stop. Sometimes it's a vague bob of the head, a slight indication to his crotch. Sometimes our eyes meet. Sometimes it's in the way he breathes. I remember one man's eyes were closed, his head slightly bowed, but I sensed that he was waiting for me. Waiting for me to go further. I did. There was only my narrow work table separating us. I reached beneath it and through his robe. His cock was hard and damp. He sighed with relief when I closed my fist around it.

With my other hand, I worked the dispenser and filled my palm with the warm, thick lotion. I coated his cock with it. He groaned again. The ring of my fingers made a slapping sound as I moved it up and down. Now and then, I caught a glimpse of his swollen, purple cockhead as I jerked his shaft with one hand and cradled his balls with the other. He was an older man—gray hair, distinguished-looking. A partner in a law firm, I think. And I was making the jism ooze out of the tip of his rich, powerful dick and drizzle down my fist.

There was another one, a high school senior getting the works—a haircut, a shave, and a manicure—for his prom. I was to give him the manicure. I wanted to get a good look at him, so I told him to get on the table, that it was customary. He didn't know any better so he did this without question. I stripped him naked and began massaging his feet, working my way up to his thighs. His cock was short and thick. It stood like a stump out of his groin. Every time my hands moved near, it would leap and jump with excitement. I did this just to tease him and to amuse myself. But it didn't last very long.

A few moments after I put my mouth on his young tool, it started to spurt like a garden sprinkler. Was this the first time anyone had sucked his cock? Maybe. He shot all over my hair, my face, my clothes. He was mortified, kept apologizing as he gathered up his robe and left in a hurry. Waiting for me in an envelope in the reception area was a crumpled bunch of dollar bills. I figured that his parents had probably given him a certain amount of money for the salon and tip, and that he contributed the rest for the special treatment from his allowance or paper route. It made me smile.

Then there's the old gentleman. Quiet, serious, widowed. I wasn't quite sure what he was after. Then I realized that what he wanted most was to talk. About his wife. I listened. I think he came to me just to be touched. Touched by another human being, but not in a sexual way. In a tender way. He came to me every week without fail, just as he did his laundry on a certain day and his grocery shopping on another. One week, after I finished buffing his nails, I pushed the table away and curled up in his lap. His hands didn't know what to do at first. Then, he just held me. We didn't move. We just breathed and held each other. After a few minutes, he eased me off his lap, stood up, and left.

The old gentleman always manages to find me no matter where I happen to be working. He makes an appointment for every Wednesday at two. Sometimes he cries. Sometimes he rocks me. Sometimes he says nothing at all. Other times, he just kisses my hand and goes. You see, it's all about hands.

Hilary's Swank on Billy the Kid
Lana Gail Taylor

Keifer's mother named him after a movie star. You know, Keifer Sutherland? I sometimes tease this Keifer that the other Keifer was practically dumped at the altar by Julia Roberts.

So this Keifer starts in on me about how my mother named me after a horse. It's not as bad as it sounds. Cassandra was my mother's first horse when she was eleven: a golden palomino mare that stood sixteen hands.

"Tall and lanky just like you turned out," mother often quipped, before adding, "Girls love horses first. Then they love boys."

I loved horses until I was thirteen and fell madly in love with Drew Barrymore. I probably liked boys, too, by then, but Drew kept me up at night cutting photos of her out of magazines—*Seventeen, Young Miss, People, Cosmopolitan*— and then tacking them to my bedroom wall. Once I smeared red lipstick across my mouth trying to look like Drew and then I held my face close to her picture, staring at the dots in the paper before pressing my mouth to her pink, glossy lips. The kiss felt flat, tasted a little bitter, but still I felt a tickle.

When I did it again, my mother walked in on me. She laughed, asking, "Cass, what are you up to?"

I answered, "I think Drew looks good in my lipstick."

Mother peered at the lip mark and then said, "I think she does, too." Then she ruffled my hair and left me alone to pursue my obsession. I don't think she was worried about it. My mother is fucking cool.

When I was fifteen and making out with boys by then, I discovered my older brother's stash of *Penthouse*. I was entranced by the colorful spreads of naked women, beautifully brazen, unfettered by clothes, and even more entranced by photos of women kissing each other's breasts and cunts. I felt the flush in my cheeks. A heart was beating in my underwear. I paged further into the thick, heavy magazine and found pictures of a male model with a muscular ass and greased-up cock poking at a woman's wide-open cunt lips.

I tucked that issue under my Madonna T- shirt and dashed back to my bedroom, locking the door. I masturbated with my pillow, then with my fingers, and then back to humping the pillow. I gawked at those pictures, concentrated on the breasts and pussies, the asses and cocks, and I came over and over again.

Of course, nothing compared to the day I discovered Drew on the cover of *Playboy*. I'm pretty sure I didn't leave my bedroom for a week.

I tell Keifer about that now and he's interested. "Do you still get hot looking at girls?"

"Sometimes."

"Like who gets you hot now?" he asks. He leans forward, elbows on the table, a smile on one side of his mouth, a glow starting to happen in his eyes.

We're eating sandwiches. Mine's a chicken breast sub with extra mayo and pickles. His is Italian meatball with tons of banana peppers falling out the sides. He scoops the peppers up with his fingers and sucks them into his mouth. I like to eat them out of his fingers, just like sometimes he enjoys cleaning mayo off my lips with his tongue.

"Drew still. Of course," I answer. "Chlöe Sevigny, Christina Ricci, and that chick from *American Beauty*."

"The blonde teenage sex kitten?"

"No way. The actress who played the sexually frustrated wife and mother."

"You're kidding."

"No way. Annette Bening is hot."

"Isn't she banging Warren Beatty?"

"I hope she's banging the living hell out of him. They're married." I sip on my diet soda, looking out the window at the sidewalk, crowds of people walking fast, impatient in the heat. It's Thursday and most people have to get back to work from their lunch break, bound to a rigid schedule, monotonous routines.

I sink my teeth into my sandwich, chew slowly, and sigh. Keifer and I fell out of bed two hours ago. And we took our sweet-ass time about it. We're both in bands. Mine's called Hilary's Swank, and his is Billy the Kid. Both bands are rock 'n' roll, but not all that great yet. Keifer plays guitar. I'm a singer. Of course, there's competition between us. Our bands play at the same bars sometimes. Last night, Billy the Kid opened for Hilary's Swank, which sort of implies that my band is better. Of course, we sparred back and forth between sets—all in good fun, of course. I love to tease Keifer. So I asked him, "Why is your guitar so big?"

Keifer eyeballed me, saying nothing.

I smiled, scratched lightly at his hand with my fingernail. "Come on. Why is it?"

"If you're going to say because my dick is small, it isn't."

"That *isn't* what I was going to say. Although I heard…." I chuckled under my breath, looked at him through my lashes.

"If you've been talking to my ex-girlfriend, then you should know she's jealous of you."

"She says your dick is only three inches long because she's jealous of *me?* How does that figure?" I shook my head, hiding a smile.

Keifer rolled his eyes at me. "Come on. You know how chicks are. They lie about guys so other chicks won't want them."

"Your ex thinks I want you?"

"Nah." Keifer shrugged. "But she might suspect I got a thing for you."

I grabbed his head then and sucked on his mouth for five minutes. When we came up for air he told me under his breath, "I wanted to do that ever since we played Taste of Colorado last spring."

That was a long time ago. Wow. Next set, I sang to him while I simulated sucking off the microphone and rubbing my hand against the seam of my pink vinyl jeans. Keifer toasted me from the audience and afterward, around three in the morning, we ended up at my place. We didn't have the patience to make out. We got to it right away, balling. His cock, which didn't feel small at all, rubbed my cunt at an angle, hitting my clit. I stuck my legs in the air, spread wide while I was panting, muttering, "Oh, oh." Keifer came first, in roughly ninety seconds, but then he kept going, staying fully cocked and rolling until I came about ninety seconds later. Then he came again. *Wow.*

We drifted off to sleep after that, his arm against my elbow and our legs overlapping, his come leaking from my cunt to the mattress. But that was OK. I wanted to sleep in the wet spot. I wanted to wake up with his semen crusted on my ass. When we woke about nine hours later, the bed smelled like our fucking, and with morning tang on our breath we kissed long and leisurely. Then we explored each other's bodies, warm from the bed sheets and sleep. His mouth slipped over my belly, my sides, my underarms, my collarbone, then my neck, chin, eyes, then back down to my tits and he sucked them. Eventually, I couldn't take it anymore. I whispered fervently, "Put your cock inside, fuck me," and it was really quite spectacular in the afternoon light, his cock—straight, pinkish-red shaft, shiny mushroom head, lots of dark blond hair behind the cute wrinkled balls that were engorging, and heck, it was at least seven inches cocked.

Hmm, nice.

Keifer sank his beauty inside me gradually while his thumb strummed my clit back and forth, slow, gentle pressure, and then in circles while I closed my eyes, sighing, going with it, holding his ass in my hands and squeezing the tightly toned muscles between my fingertips. I loved the way his ass flexed as his cock sliced wet and warm through my cunt. I couldn't help going over the top—his thumb, our rhythm. I bucked underneath his thrusts, coming, bunching up the sheets in my hands, and the whole bed was warming up moist beneath our bodies. Keifer buried his hands in my hair, his face in my neck. His breath blew on my skin, tickling hot, while his hips thrust faster, harder, and my cunt felt like soft slushing fruit sticking to his cock, sweetly satisfied, splashing over onto my legs, his balls. I circled my calves around his waist, whispered at him, "Come for me, baby," and Keifer shuddered, throwing his head back, all that long sexy hair.

Minutes later, I could feel his come leaking out with mine as we lay next to each other: the smell of sex layering the smell of sex. I loved it.

"Let's eat," Keifer suggested.

I wriggled my tongue at his cock and he grinned.

"Later," he said. "How 'bout the sandwich shop on the corner of Penn Street? Not far from here, right? We could walk."

We walked hand-in-hand. Sometimes I leaned over to kiss his cheek, which felt rough with stubble that softly scraped at my lips. Keifer's got that classically handsome face: you know, thin and chiseled, great jaw, strong. His lips are thin and pink. His blue eyes look lighter in the sunlight. So does his hair—more sandy blonde, and it's a shaggy but sexy mess. Keifer always insists, "Heavy metal hair bands are coming back, babe." And sometimes his band breaks into a rendition of Poison's "Unskinny Bop" toward the end of their third set. Keifer's too cute not to forgive. At least he hasn't busted out the spandex yet—although that would put the small-dick rumor to bed for good.

Still, I feel compelled to give him shit about hair bands. And he always comes back at me. "Chicks are fed up with ugly rock stars like Kid Rock and Fred Durst," he argued a couple of weeks ago, before our night of mad passionate love.

I wasn't sure Kid Rock was ugly. When I want to talk fu-fu-*fuckable* rock stars, I always go with the guy from Sugar Ray, or the chick from No Doubt, Gwen Stefani. Hell, I like to talk about the two of them and me at the same time.

Keifer eyeballs me when I tell him that now over sand-wiches. Then he quips, "I'm gonna fall madly in love with you."

His declaration makes me sad that my sandwich is gone. I'm still hungry. Together we eat up every last crumb of his meatball, then Keifer asks me, "Ever done a chick?"

I sit back, arms across the back of the booth, leg propped in his seat across the table, foot in his lap so that, you know, the heat from his dick can rise through his jeans and trickle across my bare ankle.

"I've done a few chicks," I tell him.

"A few? Really?" His hand starts rubbing my ankle.

"Hmmm…you know, here and there. I used to have a different bass player. She was a blonde like Drew. Named Rhiannon, after the song. We called her Ree for short. Very leggy, tight tits, really good on her bass, solid songwriter, even a vocalist sometimes, sweet. And she liked to watch. That's what she told me one night after a set. She says to me, 'Cass, I really like watching people fuck.' So I take her down Colfax, because she was from Seattle and didn't know her way around, and find one of those live sex clubs. You know, tucked out of sight and very dark inside so you can't see people's faces unless you get up to their nose." I lean across the table with big eyes for effect. Keifer pushes me playfully back.

"Go on, " he says.

"We're standing in front of the lighted stage with a small throng of people and there's a not-so-good-looking couple getting it on. The guy has this crooked dick and the chick is screaming like she's going bonkers. Maybe because his cock was bent it hit her G or something."

I shake my head, laughing. "Anyway, Ree really buys into it. She's craning her neck to see. Then she grabs me, starts feeling me up. We end up at her place, great studio downtown, and she has a *mirror* over her bed. God, I *love* looking at myself while we're getting it on. My red hair is splayed out all over the silk pillows and my green eyes are lit up like jade. She is sucking my neck, then my tits. She gives me a hickey on the left side of my right tit. I'm incredibly turned on by this point."

I pause to catch my breath, reveling in the memory, and Keifer is waiting and he gives me a nudge. "Go on."

"The next thing that happens is Ree leaves and runs into the kitchen. I stay on the bed gawking at myself, playing with my tits. The nipples look really hard and red and sexy. I've got cute little tits."

"You do."

"Hmmm.... Well, I'm expecting Ree to come back with champagne and strawberries, but she comes back with peanut butter stuff mixed with jelly. She unscrews the cap and I smell peanuts and raspberries as she rubs it all over my tits and eats it off me before spreading some more downstairs and, man, she gives good face."

I stop, smiling like a cat with a bird in its mouth. Or a chick with a mouthful of peanut butter.

"You lying about the last part?"

"Fuck, no. She gave great face. I wish I didn't have to fire her, but you know how it is. You can't fuck someone and play with her, too."

Keifer says, "Actually, I was talking about the peanut butter jelly thing."

"You liked that?"

He shrugs. Smiles a little. He liked it.

"How 'bout we buy some on the way back and make our own peanut butter and jelly sandwich?" I say. "I'll be the top."

Keifer starts rubbing my ankle harder and his hand feels warm. I sigh. And then I give him a look. "So tell me. You ever been hot for a guy?"

Keifer thinks for a moment, then answers, "Scott Weiland."

"Singer for the Stone Temple Pilots?"

He nods.

"Not a bad choice, but I thought you dug hair bands. How 'bout the cutie who used to front Warrant?" Then I can't help it. I start to laugh. *Warrant?* Tee-hee.

Keifer rolls his eyes. "OK. Stephen Dorff."

I know who he's talking about but I don't let on right away. I want to have some fun with it. So I stare at him blankly.

"The actor."

I pretend to think for a moment. "Oh. You mean Stephen Dwarf."

"No. *Dorff.*" And then Keifer catches himself and frowns, waving me off. "Fuck you, Cass. He's not a dwarf."

"Dude, that guy is like five foot two. *Dwarf.*" I start laughing again. And then I ask, "Fuck me? You promise?"

He's still pissed.

I rub my foot in his lap so that it's getting his dick, and I can feel it's already half-hard. Guys *do* turn him on. Who can blame him? I mean, Stephen Dorff—come on, the guy *is* short, but he's hot looking, especially when he played the sleazy little vampire in *Blade*.

I tell Kiefer that. To make him feel better. Then I say, "I'd like watching a guy suck your dick. Has that ever happened before?"

Keifer nods. "On the road. This guy was in another band. He sort of reminded me of...." Keifer eyeballs me. "Let's just say he was good looking. And he was cool. Fucking kick-ass drummer, too."

"A drummer? Hmm...." I rub my foot a little harder against the erection in his pants. His hand around my ankle tightens again.

"Yeah. We have a few beers after the show and we talk and I get this vibe off him. Like he wants to say something but won't. I'm not sure how we end up in his van. We're just there. We don't say anything. He opens my pants and goes for my dick. I'm a little freaked out at first. My cock isn't hard in his hands until he goes down on it. He's sucking me off. I can't make him out in the dark, and the van is quiet. *Everything* is dark and quiet, almost like the fucking world has stopped, and all I hear is my breathing, this guy breathing, and the sound his mouth makes on my cock. I sit back and let it roll. It's good—his warm mouth, all the saliva, the way he uses his tongue. My cock is fucking granite. It almost hurts, and I feel kind of clammy, maybe freaked out still, a little, but man, I shoot off a couple of mouthfuls at least."

I stare at him, *stare,* and my clit's got a fucking boner. I swear to God. "That just turned me on," I tell him. "Even better than my story." I rub his dick harder with my foot. It's fully cocked now, straining against the seam of his pants. I want to crawl under the table and suck him off. Step up to bat and beat out his mysterious male lover. And fuck, if I don't need to masturbate right now, or get fucked fast, or man, if he would go down on me and try to top Ree with his tongue. That would be *something else.*

I manage to sit still in my seat. "Tell me another thing, Keifer. Did you give this guy head?"

"Nah, but he wanted me to. He was busting to blow after getting me off."

I push my foot harder against his crotch, and he moves his hips a little so that his cock presses the arch, my toes wriggling. "Wasn't ready to go down on a guy, I guess. But I let him rub his cock against my ass through my pants and he finally unloaded. Fuck, there was so much guy jizz all over that van, and my pants." Keifer laughs. "He had to loan me another pair."

I stand up from the table. My clit is tickling and it won't stop. Now my nipples are standing up inside my T-shirt, too, and to add to the aching tickle in my nipples is the fact that the cotton is rubbing my sensitive skin right there, ahhh…. I sound breathless when I say to Keifer, "We're skipping the grocery store for peanut butter and jelly. I need to get you back in bed. Right. Fucking. Now."

• • •

Sometime later, Hilary's Swank is playing a gig. The band breaks into a trashy groove and I sing, "Don't call me Mrs. Clinton, call me *Msss*…. I don't smoke cigars. But I do eat Bush. Hey, ey, ey…."

Billy the Kid has the week off, but Keifer is in the crowd tonight and he's giving me the thumbs up, wiggling his tongue between his fingers and grinning, laughing it up. It's hard to get out of bed anymore with him in it. I think he moved in last week. Still, I'm determined to get better as a musician, so I rehearse with Hilary's Swank almost every day, and I'm writing new songs all the time. I want to write one about Keifer, a love song. It's called "Hilary's Swank on Billy the Kid." I got another one, too. It's about Keifer and Stephen Dorff. Which makes me smile while I'm singing to this crowd tonight. It's all so fucking happening. My band is kicking ass. The crowd looks wild. They're all screaming and getting it on.

And then I hear my man over the top of all this other mayhem. He's standing on a table, hollering, "Drew Barrymore forever, baby!"

I fucking love that guy so much.

Go

Jen Collins

My girlfriend sees that look in my eyes again tonight. We are out at dinner, sharing a lovely meal of avocado *maki*, California rolls, and plum wine. Instead of focusing my attention on the way Laura's lovely lips wrap around my fingers as I feed her each bite of sushi, I am wondering how I can hook our waiter into the men's room to give him a proper tip.

Laura always sees my wandering eyes, no matter how good I think I'm being. She says, with a grin, "Why don't you hit the Masque tonight?" I try to act cool in response, but she can see my cheeks flush in anticipation. I pay the bill quickly, leaving the indifferent waiter too large a tip just so that I don't have to wait for change. I leave Laura at her car with a long kiss, listening to her delighted laughter following me as I walk through the steamy night toward the club.

Laura never comes with me when I go out on nights like these—she'd blow my cover. She loves to hear my stories when I get home, though. And tonight, I grin to myself, will be no exception.

As I pay the cover, I ignore the smirk of the man taking my

money. He knows me, and knows why I come here.

"On the prowl, Murph?"

"Shut up, Jim." I keep my eyes down. If I meet his, I'll surely smile. My smile always gives me away.

When I first came to the Masque a year or so ago, Jim simply saw a piece of fresh meat. He looked me up and down and started with his best come-on lines. A quick glance at my ID and he did a double take. I met his shocked eyes when he looked back up at me—my skinny hips and broad shoulders, my cropped hair and squarish jaw. I put a finger to my lips, returned Jim's confused smile with my own, and took my ID back. I slipped into the crowd while he was busy reconciling what he had been thinking about doing to me, and the "me" I turned out to be.

Later that night, Jim watched, mouth hanging open, as I hurried the boy I wanted, a boy Jim recognized from the gay men's community, out the door and over to the side of the building. Luckily, Jim didn't get the chance to say anything before I got this guy's pants down.

Now, when I come in, Jim gives me a knowing look. I think I get more action at the club than he does—and from men he considers to be in his arena, not mine. Maybe sometime we'll meet in the real world and discuss desire and identity over a couple of beers. But until then, I count on him to keep my secret. For whatever reason, he does.

I make my way to the bar and order tequila, turning down the offer of salt and lime. I leave a five-spot for the tab, down the shot in a single swallow, and lean back against the bar. The drink settles warmly around my cunt, relaxing my hips and thighs. Oiling the machinery.... I glance around to see who's here tonight. No one I recognize yet. That's good. It wouldn't do to be recognized too early.

There are lots of pretty boys here tonight. But I don't want just any gay boy. I'm looking for a boy who might not ever imagine looking at a girl. Until he finds himself grinding up against me, all of a sudden not so sure if I'm a boy or a girl, but hoping that maybe he's just missing something as he rides his knee between my legs.

I need to relax a little more, and get a better view of the club. So I move out onto the dance floor and nestle into a corner. I scan the dancers, and then catch sight of the one I'd like to catch tonight. An Asian boy, he's got cropped black hair that's gelled down so slick it looks wet. Or maybe that's sweat. His short-sleeved, print button-down shirt is unbuttoned and untucked, and he wears a smooth white cotton undershirt that fits snugly over firm chest muscles. Blue jeans slouch on his hips. White socks and black Docs complete the gay boy uniform. It gets me every time.

There's a particular kind of flirting one has to do when trying to attract the attention of a gay boy—and one is not, strictly speaking, another gay boy. At first I just dance. I find a niche in the music I can fit my body into, a rhythm that moves me around the floor. The tequila helps at first. But pretty soon, I've sweated the alcohol right out, and it's only my own desire moving my ass. Then I begin breathing harder, because the song is so good and I can't stop to rest. My mouth is open a bit and my eyes are closed. I run my hands up along my neck to wipe off the sweat that's running there, and I open my eyes as I do so. Maybe he's looking at me. I don't check. I close my eyes again and keep moving. In my imagination, he finds this intriguing and so looks at me, every once in a while, to see if I'm still sweating like that.

Now, if a guy doesn't have an itch for something a little different, I'm not going to get even the time of day from him. Some gay men only go for butch ones. But then there are queer boys looking for someone more along my line: a boy who could be a girl maybe, but then is a boy again. Frankly, I like those boys, too. *And* those girls. This boy I've picked out tonight appears to like those kinds of boys too, because he's watching me and trying to figure me out. I don't think he's here with anyone, which is a plus: I don't need him to have a friend lean over and point out my chromosomal makeup.

The DJ switches from hardcore techno to something with a little more bass, a rhythm you can almost sit on. This is the music that gets people coupled, gets 'em close. I cock my head toward my boy, and find him looking at me. We begin dancing together, although we're still several feet apart. It takes a while to move in until we're touching. I need him to be hooked by that time. I have my hands back behind me, and my hips thrust forward. He's definitely turned on—I can make out his arousal, even in the dim and flashing lights of the club. His eyes are half-closed and his lips are full. I'm taller than he is by several inches. I tilt my head to look down at him, moving in a little closer with every rotation of my hips, which I swipe along his thigh. One more step, and my thigh will rest between his legs. I learned this move seducing women, and yet I always manage to use it when I'm working on a boy. Habit, I guess.

My thigh presses up against a solid hard-on. I glance at him and let a little smile creep across my face. He is not feeling a hard-on of any sort. He looks a little bewildered, but then I push up against his dick, riding him on my thigh, and his bewilderment evaporates into the shock of sensation. Maybe he has no friends here. Maybe he's not from around here. Maybe we're just getting into this song. The club is hot. The light is low, so low that he can imagine no one can see him. If he thought I was a boy, he might rationalize that everyone else probably does too.

We continue dancing, and I urge us back farther into the corner. I rest a hand on the thigh between his legs as I move. My fingers press up against his dick with each rotation. His cheek brushes up against mine, lips near my ear. He gasps each time I touch him. Then he brings his hands around and rests them on my ass. We move in sync, and he moves one of his legs forward to press against me, against my cunt, until I gasp myself. I turn my hand up and cup his dick. I want to feel him inside me, and he knows it. What's more, maybe worse, is that he wants it, too.

He leans into me and I hear his soft, urgent voice close to my ear. "I'm not straight."

"I'm not either," is all I manage to reply before his hands are on my face and he kisses me. His transgression is secured with my words. Another queer knows what this means for him.

"I've never, you know…" he starts. I can see he's flushed. "I never have…."

"You'll figure it out," I say. I take his hand and lead him back behind the DJ booth. The smell of sweat and sex is over-powering here, the music just as loud as out front.

There's a hand against my chest as soon as I part the cur-tain to the back room. I make a face at Mack, trying to convey how badly I need to get by. "It's me, Mack," I say impatiently. "Let us through."

"Goddamnit, Murphy," he says, waving us through. "Leave some for the rest of us."

I take note of my boy's shocked face as we pass out of the light. Guess he didn't know this part of the club existed. He catches a brief glimpse of bodies together before the curtain closes and we're shrouded in darkness, the heavy bass under-side of the music, and other people's moans.

I get him against a wall. With a hand resting on his chest, I unbuckle his belt and open his fly. He helps, pulling his very hard cock out of his pants. He gives a barely audible cry as I sink down into a squat. I have a condom out of my own pocket and am smoothing it over his dick by the time he fishes out his own.

Ignoring his surprised look, I lick under his dick head and then swallow the tip. I move slowly, taking the length of him into my mouth, then letting his dick ease back out again. After a few moments of this, he clasps his hands around my head, and begins to fuck my mouth. I love when they're this horny.

My hands fit snugly around his hips, and I rest them there. My own sex swells with arousal at being taken this way. As a bonus, my clit rubs against the seam of my jeans in this position. His dick fills my mouth, and he hits the back of my throat with each thrust. I wrap my tongue around the base to make this as smooth as possible. But the boy wants to come, so I sit back on my haunches and let him take over the ride. He lets out a loud moan, and I open my throat to his sharp, impatient thrusts as he shoots.

He pulls out of my mouth and yanks me to my feet while removing the rubber; his swiftness surprises me. Guess he's comfortable now. He presses me up against the wall, just the way I did him, only my back is now to his front. I press my cheek to the cool concrete, watching him out of the corner of my eye.

Using his teeth, he tears open his condom packet. I busy my hands with unfastening my jeans. I start to shift them down my hips, but he swats my hands away. He puts one hand on the back of my jeans and jerks downward a couple of times, until my ass is exposed. My hands are flat against the wall, holding me up.

He whispers in my ear again, but with the pounding of my heart and the throb of the music, I can't make out all his words: "...fuck you" and "...way I like to..." and so on. I shove my ass and thighs back into him, shifting in little circles, to entice him in. Looking over my shoulder, I watch as he spits into his hand, then runs his fingers along my ass, wetting the hole that's not wet already. He jerks his cock back to rigidity right up next to my ass, then roughly smoothes the condom over it. I move my left hand down to his ass and pull him toward me. He places his free hand at the base of my spine, steadying me.

He presses the head of his dick against my asshole. I push back slightly, meeting this intimate touch. I grab his tiny hipbone, indicating: *Wait, don't move.* I ease away from his dick, then back again, fucking myself onto him. Once the head is in, I move my hand from his hip to my cunt and rub some of my own lube back onto his dick, slicking it all over the shaft. I bring my wet hand to my clit and then turn my head just a little, so that he can see my lips, not so cool anymore.

"Go."

He jerks his hips swiftly, and manages to fuck his dick fully into me with a few solid strokes. I throw my head back and moan. I tell him to work it, tell him to fuck me. "Oh, shit, yeah," I'm moaning. "Fuck me." Whatever I have to say to get him to keep going. He grabs my waist with both hands and fucks me hard, showing no mercy. I work my fingers fast and furious on my clit, with legs spread so that I can get in good. When I feel the clench of orgasm gathering in me, I close my eyes. I turn my face back toward him, and, with some effort for coherence, I talk to him so that he knows it's coming.

"Keep it going, baby. Don't stop. Oh, God, yeah—don't...don't stop. Please don't stop."

He manages to hear my pleas in spite of the rest of the noise enveloping us. His right hand is off my hip now and over my breast, fumbling for the part he recognizes. He finds a nipple and squeezes it through my shirt. Oh, God. The added sharpness of sensation throws me over the edge. I come hard, howling and grunting through clenched teeth. As I shudder through my orgasm, contracting my ass around him, my boy's dick swells again. With a few more hard thrusts, he gives a short yelp like someone in pain, and I feel the spasms of his orgasm, too. He leans against me and drops his hands to his side, both of us panting and moaning. With his dick shoved clear up into me, we are just about as close as two people can get. I don't even know his name.

Jen Collins

We stand there for a minute, recovering, him against my back and me against the wall. His cheek is against my neck, and I feel the sweet smoothness of his sticky, sweaty skin. Gently, he pulls away from me, and then pulls out. After two hard orgasms, he's finally softening.

I work against him, easing forward. My ass is gonna be sore on the walk home tonight. He removes the condom, knots the end, and tosses it on the floor with the rest. They must have to hose this place down with bleach every night.

We each pull up and refasten our jeans, standing stupidly in the afterglow of anonymous orgasm. He looks to me for the etiquette. I lean in and whisper, "Thanks, baby." I kiss him on the neck (kisses on the lips get me too turned on all over again, and I need to get out of here). I turn and head out of the back room. I don't want him to think too much about what he just did, or get into a conversation with him about what all of this means.

Walking out with a bit more swagger than I went in with, I give Mack a wink and pass into the club. Mack, this older bear of a man, shakes his head at me with a hard grin, and looks back to see where my companion went. I move around to the other side of the DJ booth, and wait for a minute. My boy does not follow. Snagged, probably by Mack. Figures. Mack always goes for sloppy seconds. Next time I see that boy, my guess is that he'll only remember me for showing him the way into that particular bit of heaven. I hope he has more rubbers.

I walk back to the bar, easing my used ass gently onto a stool. I accept the bartender's offer of a glass of water. I'd like to dance for a few songs, but I'm exhausted and I still have to walk a ways to get home. More importantly, I'll have to tell the tale to Laura, who will want me to demonstrate certain key parts of the evening.

The DJ switches to another heavy bass line, which I take as my cue. Before I walk out, I scan the floor once more.

There he is—my boy dancing with Mack, who must've found someone to cover the entrance to the backroom. I manage to catch the boy's eye, and he grins at me, the way you might smile at a good friend. The look Mack gives me is of another caliber altogether. I smile back at them both, and head out into the night, home toward my girl.

Extracurriculars

Joy VanNuys

All that drunken culinary students want to talk about is how sexy they are. As if it makes up for the backaches, the lousy pay, and the constant smell of fried food that makes strangers back away on the subway. Because, see, food is love, and love is sex, and since we can cook, someone will love us. Or at least someone will say, "Oh, you're a chef?" and go home with us just to find out what a chef has for breakfast. Cheerios, usually. Sometimes with milk, as a garnish.

When I step out of class into the air, the last thing I want to do is eat, though I can feel that ache in the pit of my stomach that says all I had today was one bite each of broccoli puree, carrot timbale, sweet-potato gratin. The first thing I want is a drink. The next is a cigarette. And the next is a pair of arms, rocking me, saying it'll be OK, I was good today. A pair of lips, opening mine, tasting me, giving me an "A" for texture, moisture, saltiness. A hand full of fingers, strong from endless knife drills, opening my thighs, sinking deep into my body, branding me as someone's.

For the first half-hour at the bar, the kitchen still pounds in our brains—food, food, food. I tell them how butchering the bunny made tears come to my eyes, and Tony says he almost puked when he had to clean the kidneys. Frank and Juan argue over whose plating was more inspired for the paupiettes of sole, while Rose fights off boys who come over to guess her age, since her body says seventeen but her eyes say forty-two. We feed the waitress grilled ostrich with our fingers, and she brings us free drinks. These are my brothers and sisters, and I have bandaged their oyster shell gashes, snapped latex gloves over fingers boned like lamb shanks, smelled their skin sautéing to a light golden brown. Siblings or not, there's not a single one I'd kick out of my bed.

Around the third drink I start to notice what he looks like in real clothes, how pretty her eyes are when they're wide with booze. Wives, boyfriends, sexual preferences, fade into the background and the air gets palpably thicker.

"So, you've been around. Which is better, men or women?" Frank asks me, as he leans in to rub Rose's shoulder blades.

"Women," Rose and I say together, smiling into each other's eyes, then looking away quickly.

"How can that be? What do you need, a cucumber or something?"

"It's called finesse, Frank. When you've got finesse, who needs cock?" Rose tells him.

"But, girl, what can you do without a little of this?" he asks, shaking his thin hips up and down. Frank wants sex so bad, every minute of the day. In class, he dry-humps me, whispers "I want you" in my ear, then giggles like a lunatic and goes back to the flounder he was filleting. Despite the obvious distractions, the guy can cook. He shakes Tabasco and cayenne onto every plate, and it all tastes smooth and warm, never too hot. The first day of class, I clicked on that face, that ass, just like every other woman in the room. Now he's familiar enough that I can hump him back, most days, with barely a spark.

"To me," I say, "it's the difference between being filled and being opened. It all depends on what you need on that particular day."

"It's like…well, women are oysters, and men are meatloaf," Rose says. "Like men are satisfying and warm and homey—wait, that's women. So women are meatloaf and oysters, and men are hotdogs. Like, they're not good for you, and they're made of all kinds of disgusting crap, but you love them anyway."

I stand with Frank, at Gray's Papaya Hut. We butt heads as we fight for the single straw in our large bucket of papaya juice. Our fingers meet at the mustard pump. Three hot dogs, two gone in an instant. He puts one end of the last hot dog in his mouth, and I attack the other end, biting and chewing. Soon our lips are touching; our mouths still filled with meat and bun. We swallow and kiss. His cock is insistent, pressing against me through his jeans. His eyes are shocking blue, just like mine. I have promised him a friendly lay, but this is wrong, like balling-your-older-brother wrong. I run my fingertips over the leather of his jacket, trying to conjure up a fantasy, but his breath on my neck is puppy dogs and comfort. I walk him around the corner; there are still alleyways in New York City, if you know where to look. I unzip him, gently take his penis in my hand and caress it, moving up and down. It is lovely, smooth and pink, and I lick my lips, wondering how dirty I'd get if I knelt, whether he is worth a few scratches on my kneecaps. His hands move to my zipper, but I say, "No. Let me do you." As the word do leaves my mouth, he spurts, first into my fingers, then high in an arc onto the brick wall. He shudders, holds me tight, and I wipe my hand on his jeans, pretending that I'm stroking his ass. He licks my ear, and I shudder inside, just a little. I love him, in a Christmas morning way.

" 'Women are oysters' is an anatomical cliché," I say, and as the words come out, I know I have given myself away again, put my Columbia education up for ridicule. "I mean, just because oysters look like pussy, and feel like pussy, and taste like pussy...."

"Jesus, that's hot," Sean says, from behind me.

"I didn't know you were coming tonight," I say. If Frank is my brother, Sean is the hot cousin I always wanted to fuck.

"And I didn't know you ate pussy."

"Well, I...." But the moment is gone, because Rose is talking again, and when Rose talks, I am left in the dust. The girl is electric, the fastest one in the class, all ninety pounds of her flying from fridge to stove to plate. Somehow in this room, where the machismo test centers on whether you can carry thirty pounds of spitting veal bones on a 500-degree tray across a slippery floor without flinching, she has attained excellence through grace. Watch her body, ridiculous in its too-large white jacket, baggy checked pants, twirling and dancing as she sautés. Her hat cannot contain her hair, which springs into action at the slightest hint of humidity. Sometimes when I look at her, I have to bite my thumb, hard, to keep from I don't know what.

"The thing is, women are just so beautiful. Their bodies are so lush, so curvy," Rose says, and all eyes are on me, on the cleavage that is the only compensation for being as chubby as I am at this point in my life.

We are taking a bath in Dead Sea salts, in her massive claw-foot tub. I am shy, and try to stay under the soapsuds, but she stretches back, showing me her small, perfect breasts, her dark nipples rising. I wash her arms, carefully rubbing the distinct, sore muscles. "Turn around," she tells me, and I move until I feel her kiss on the back of my neck. She fills her hands with lather and begins to work my breasts from behind, squeezing and stroking them. Each is more than one skinny hand can handle, but she tries hard, milking and caressing me. My nipples slip from her soapy fingers, beg to be pinched, but there is nothing demanding here, nothing not yielding and soft. I turn to see her gorgeous face, and feel her fingers between my legs, my wrinkles and folds opening for her. To my fingers, she feels the same. The same as touching myself, as fresh-shucked oysters, as the thing I love best. "God, God, God," I come, and stretch and smile. I step out of the tub, pull her to a seated position on the edge. She is briny, metallic, buttery-smooth and ridged all at once. I lick my lips, lick her lips, searching for a hint of lemon juice. I suck and swallow and hold her hips firm till she is limp in my arms.

"Curvy is good," Sean says. "I like women who have something to them. No offense, Rose baby."

He is no slight thing himself. He's about six-three and solid, looks like he played football in high school. He has meaty arms, thick hands. Hugging him would be like embracing a warm, lightly furred mountain.

"Meatloaf," I say, without thinking.

"Geez, thanks a lot," Sean says. "I cut my hair, take off fifty pounds, and I'm still getting that?"

"No, not the person. I was just thinking about something we said earlier, about meatloaf being homey and satisfying and nurturing...." And, I think, so sweet to fuck. It will be so sweet to take you into my bed, to see the map of Ireland on your thick cock, to feel small in your strong arms.

My jeans are lost under the bed somewhere. I am lying on my belly, his fingers are fumbling, working my bra off. I help him, reaching back to flip off the hooks. His hands move down, give my ass a light spank, and then rub me up and over, integrating all my parts, reminding me what this body is for.

I have not seen him naked yet, have only heard his T-shirt come off, his jeans unzip. He gently pulls me onto all fours, my ass in the air, and I feel his warm skin on mine as he bends over me. His cock explores the insides of my thighs, tickling them, and I resist the urge to move my legs together, press down hard on him, just to get an idea of what he's got. My hand snakes back between our legs, he pulls back, not letting me touch him. I hear the slithery sound that comes next—the crinkle of a condom wrapper. Then, a miracle: I am a virgin again, too tight to let him in. Bit by bit, he works his cock inside me, and I feel myself opening. Every millimeter is a spasm, each tiny thrust a spark. His hands hold my hips, reach around to cup my hanging breasts, but every nerve is dead except the ones in my cunt, the ones that are fucking him now. Grinding my hips backward, I take it all at last, proud that I've made it this far, sorry that that's all there is. As he moves back, I think, "Bat out of Hell," and wonder what's in the fridge.

"That's the thing," Tony says. "Sometimes you make something so good, so hot and juicy, that it's simply too good to eat. Instead, you want to buy it a drink, take it to bed with you, and make love to it all night long."

The image of Tony with his cock buried in a plate of eggplant parmigiana is enough to shock me slightly sober, to realize that: one, my baby is waiting for me at home, keeping my bed warm, and two, I have soaked through my jeans.

In the cab, I check to make sure that my bag isn't coated with rosemary-ginger butter, that the filet mignon I snagged is safe and sound. I muffle the sound of my zipper going down, and reach down to tease my clit a little, thinking about what a chef has for breakfast. Jelly donuts, mac and cheese, salami on white. Jerk off, a long hot shower, and it's time to go out and do it all again.

Full Service
Erica Dumas

It's about two in the morning when it happens. It's been a long night: ten jobs and a couple of full-service in the booths at the Rab. Things are slowing down here since the cops came by a few minutes ago, scattering the whores and johns like pigeons. I decide to hit Lucky's. I tried there earlier, and that bouncer Moose wouldn't even let me in the door. But I know Mikey takes over at two, and he'll usually let me in the back for twenty bucks unless his boss is working. And from what I hear, usually on Saturday his boss is on a coke binge in some hotel somewhere, avoiding his wife. Sometimes I have to flirt a little, but Mikey always gives in.

The bouncer at the Rab looks me up and down as I leave; he's probably just glad I had the good sense to hide out until the pigs left. I pass from the smell of semen and Clorox into the smell of cigarettes and urine, walk up 42nd Street toward Lucky's, putting my sunglasses on to block out the neon. I smell the sharp chemical plastic smell coming out of the alley behind the 24-hour deli. My heart pounds and I get short of breath. *Fuck,* I tell myself, *Just don't think about it.*

Remember why you're clean: so that you can finish writing your play and move to L.A. You'll never get to L.A. if you keep getting high, and you'll be a stupid whore forever instead of a screenwriter, and Nicolas Cage will never be in your movies. I don't give a shit, I want to go back into the alley and beg for a hit, but then I remember Janie standing over me and telling me how disappointed she is. I'm not really convinced, though, until I remember her standing over me with the curling iron and telling me if I get high ever again she'll fucking kill me. I hurry on up to Lucky's.

Mikey doesn't even make me flirt with him, just palms the twenty and waves me in the back door. I slip into the shadows, smelling the sharp spunk and cleaning fluid. I have to take my sunglasses off, which I hate doing. I perch them on my head and walk past the aisles of peepshow booths, looking around. No way I'd turn a trick in one of these; those fucking strippers will narc on you in a second, because you're cutting into their tips and they're as desperate for their cash as I am for mine. But the video booths are wide open—a quarter a minute and ten times easier to get a guy's dick hard when there isn't some nineteen-year-old anorexic watching him. Most guys don't like to be watched.

I see you as I turn the corner and slip into the video section. You're standing under a poster of the twenty features currently being offered—four straight, four barely legal, four anal, four gay, four kink. Fuck, this never happens to me; I never lose my panties over a potential trick like this. Not that I'm complaining—I like it, sure, but nothing prepared me to spend tonight having my jaw dropped by the prettiest fucking biker boy I've ever seen. How old are you, nineteen? I mean, I know I'm nineteen but I'm used to guys twenty, thirty years older than me, at least. My stomach's churning and my heart's pounding like it was when I smelled the crack out in the alley. And that's when you see me looking at you, and our eyes meet. Your eyes are big, steel-blue, hard. Your little goatee curves a bit as you look me up and down. You smile and my knees go weak. It's like a surge of electricity goes through me and I know I'll give you a fucking freebie if you don't want to come up with the cash. Jesus, with eyes like that, I should be paying *you*.

Like I'm in a dream, I start down the hall, trying to be cool. You just keep looking at me, no matter how many times I look down, and my pussy feels so wet I could almost believe it really is. I totter on my heels, feeling your eyes cover my legs, hips, tits, face. I can't even look up at you for fear all the blood will rush out of my head.

Instead, I look at your body, your nipples hard under the white T-shirt, your feet sturdy in heavy motorcycle boots, your chiseled legs in those skintight leather pants, the outline of your cock making my mouth water. Fuck, it's big; it almost looks hard already. I pray to God you're not gay; I never see straight guys wear pants that tight. Especially not at Lucky's, where you're lucky if your trick's pants are denim and not polyester.

I walk up to you, not knowing what to say. I lean close, smiling, feeling my head spin as I take a breath and smell you, cologne and sharp male sweat, cigarettes and whiskey. "Want a date?" I ask, and my voice breaks, squeaking. I feel your hand on my hip, pulling me close, and I melt into you.

"How much?" you ask.

Fifty bucks is the asking for full service, but I don't do full service, so I usually ask thirty for a blow. I've let it go for ten, but I usually don't have to; I'm young enough and pretty enough that guys are usually OK with twenty. But you—I'm terrified you'll say no, so I just whisper "Fifteen," ashamed of myself that I want it so bad.

"For full service?" You sound incredulous, like you can't believe a whore as pretty as me would give it up so easy. Your lips are against my neck, your hot whiskey breath caressing my ear. I can feel my pussy throbbing. God, I'll give you anything, but I can't give you that.

I don't know what to say. Finally I stammer, "I don't do full service."

"You'll do it with me," you say, and my whole body sinks into you as I hear your throaty rumble in my ear. "I'll give you twenty."

My heart is pounding, "It's fifty," I blurt out. "Fifty for full service." I know you'll turn me down, just know it, and maybe you'll settle for a blowjob. If not, maybe I'll lose you, but I simply can't give you full service. Janie would kill me, sure as if I smoked again.

"Done," you say, and I feel your hand on my ass, squeezing through the skintight spandex skirt, maybe noticing that I haven't got a stitch on underneath. "Like, I'm going to let a sweet piece of ass like you get away?" Then you kiss me, and I don't kiss, not even Janie, I never kiss, but my lips slip apart and your tongue thrusts into me like it's your hard cock. Tears form in my eyes; I haven't been kissed since I was a kid, a little kid. Power surges through me as your tongue plumbs my mouth; I feel it in my heart, my belly, my crotch, the tips of my toes.

And then you're half pushing me, half guiding me, down the hall to the far end, where I see the Preview Room is open. I almost can't believe it; I've never been fucked in here; it's twenty fucking dollars for an hour, for Christ's sake. Nobody ever does me in here; I'm more used to the cramped little quarter slots, me with my knees in little puddles of cum. I've never even *seen* the inside of the Preview Booth.

You put twenty bucks in the slot, and the intercom crackles. "Which title do you want?"

"Biker Bitches," you say. "Part 8."

"We only have part 7."

"Fine," you say, and the door clicks open. You don't have to push me inside, but you do, just a little—insistent, but reasonably polite, which I'm not used to. It's dark inside, pitch dark, and it smells more like cum and sweat and cigarettes than it does like Clorox; I wonder how many hours—or days—it's been since they cleaned in here. When you close the door you grab me and whirl me around and shove me up against it, and the floor is so slippery that I lose my balance and I would fall if you didn't catch me and hold me, your body against mine, against the door. You reach behind me and shut the bolt.

"What's your name?" you ask.

"Eden," I tell you. "My name's Eden."

"Where you from?"

"Forty-Second Street," I say.

"Hmm, a fifteen-dollar whore with a sense of humor," you say. "I like that."

"Fifty," I say nervously. "It was fifty."

"I know."

Your mouth fuses to mine, your tongue pushing in deeper than before, and I feel it harder than ever, surging through me, making me want to give myself to you, give everything there is to give. When you pull back, just a little, I can almost feel your lips hovering an inch from mine, and I breathe your whiskey-smoke breath like it was coming from a glass pipe. You take my hands and push them back against the door, holding me like you've got me tied there, like you've got me tied to a bed the way Janie likes to do, only this time I want it, I want it more than anything. I want you to shackle my hands to the wall of this preview booth and never fucking let me go, go anywhere except up against your body.

"I...I don't kiss," I say weakly, hardly even able to find the breath to speak.

"You're kissing *me*," you say, and kiss me again, hard, your teeth nipping my lower lip. Your tongue almost reaches the back of my throat, and I feel more open than I ever have. I'm scared shitless, not that you'll hurt me, but that I won't be able to go back—that Janie's weak kisses won't be enough for me after the taste of a real man's cock.

"I'm not allowed," I finally say when you let me. "I'm not allowed to kiss."

"You are now," you say, and kiss me again, and then there's the sound of a click as the viewscreen goes on, and blue light floods the booth. You pull away, and I look around. Fuck, this is the Ritz-Carlton as far as I'm concerned. It's a good ten feet by ten feet, almost like a real room, and there's a real fucking loveseat, its blood-red upholstery crusted and rubbed raw, but still, it's there. I know I'm not going to be sitting in it, but still. And then you push me into the loveseat, sit down next to me, your hip pushing against mine, as you put your arms around me and start to kiss me again. The blue light goes out all of a sudden, and the movie starts in—moans and gasps and cheesy music, girls asking to get fucked in the ass.

"Fifty bucks," I say weakly. "I already told you, fifty bucks."

But you've already got your hand in the pocket of my little clear-plastic jacket, the one I like to wear because it shows everything off, and I feel the crisp bill in there. I take it out and look at it—it's really a fifty. I haven't seen a fifty in forever, and you're the first guy in five years who's paid me without having to be asked more than once. That almost makes me cream, but it's mostly the feel of your hands all over me that really makes me go crazy, makes me want to get to my knees on the slippery floor and take your cock in my mouth. Your hands work their way under my spandex tube top, pulling it up; you pinch my nipples as you kiss my neck, making me shiver. I feel your hot mouth on my tits, your teeth biting and grinding, something I love so much and Janie never does to me. Not that she does anything to me, anymore. I feel my bare legs against your leather ones, and you lean hard against me and jam your knee up between my spread thighs. I feel your leather-clad knee against my crotch, and I moan. Fuck, I can't believe I told you I'd give you full service. My only hope is to get you off with my mouth and then maybe you won't want to fuck me after all.

The previews end. I hear the roar of Harleys, the throb of techno music. I've got to suck your cock or I'm going to go crazy, and besides, every instant I wait it's more likely you're going to put your hands up my skirt and feel how wet I really, really am. And then you'll know I'd turn this trick for free if I had to. I fish a condom out of my jacket pocket. As if you can read my mind, you take my hand and grab the condom, toss it away into the darkness.

"We don't need to use a condom," you say, and I can't bear to say anything. Janie would kill me, but I don't care. I'm going to feel your cock inside me, bare and raw and naked and slick, and there's nothing I can do to stop myself. I breathe deeply of your scent as it mingles with the cum and the smoke and the thick sounds of fucking and moaning from the screen.

Your hand slides up my knee, and I struggle against you for a moment, as you hold me down. You are not going to let me get away, and you're much, much stronger than I am. Your hand slips between my legs; I force them closed and whisper, "Let me suck you a little, first."

"A shy whore? Playing hard to get?"

"I just want to suck your cock a little," I say coquettishly, and you let go. I slip out of your grasp and drop to my knees, feeling them slip a little in puddles of fluid; I have to keep them spread wide to get stable. I put my face in your crotch and start to work your belt open with my fingers. You fish a pack of cigarettes out of your leather jacket and shake two cigarettes out of the pack.

You light both and hand me one. I've been wanting a cigarette all night, but Janie gets pissed off if I spend my money on smokes.

I feel my whole body on fire as I look at the burning cherry of the cigarette. I ask it: "You don't...um, you don't have any rock, do you?"

You shake your head. "I don't do drugs," you say. "Except whiskey and cigarettes. That crack stuff'll kill you."

I nod. "I'm trying to get clean," I say. I take a puff, two, three, and then hold the cigarette out to the side as I get your belt open and unbutton your leather pants. They're thick leather, but well-worn, buttery. I get your zipper down and there it is, bulging out from your jockeys, hard already. I feel a wave of satisfaction, flattered for some reason by the fact that you're hard before I start to suck you. That makes me want you more, so bad my mouth is watering, so bad a little trail of drool runs down my chin and dribbles onto your balls. My mouth descends on your cock and I take it almost all the way down my throat before the taste hits me: pussy, fresh, mixed with rubber. It sends a surge through me as I remember what it's like to eat out a woman—Jamie doesn't let me do her like that—and I want it all of a sudden. I want to taste more cunt, except that it hits me, in a flood, that I'm tasting it on your cock, another woman's cunt on your cock, and I'm jealous, bitterly jealous, almost angry. Even that can't stop me from wanting it, but I let your cock slip out of my mouth.

"You've been fucking already tonight," I breathe, looking up at you.

"That's right."

Which is when it hits me—the rubber smell, the sharp plastic taste, somehow different than condoms. For a second I think you're already wearing one, a rubber, and since I can't see in the flickering fuck-light from the screen, it takes me putting your cock back in my mouth before my eyes go wide and I realize it, all of a sudden.

I look up at you, my mouth still full.

You look down, your eyes flashing with the light from the pale flesh dancing on the screen.

"Do you mind?" you ask me.

And it hits me, hard, the longing in my pussy, the heat of my hunger for your cock, the sudden need to feel you fuck me, fuck me hard in every hole I have. I should have known; I really should have known. No man is that gorgeous. No man can make me cream like this. No man can make me think about giving full service on my knees in the preview booth. Breathing hard, my mouth still around the head of your cock, I wrestle my hand down into your tight leather pants and feel it, your slit, nestled behind the little metal ring with its leather backing, the thick flange of your cock with its ridge positioned just right for your clit. I could almost swear I taste your cock leaking pre-cum, but it's your pussy I feel juicing on my hand. I slip one finger inside and you sigh, pressing your cock up into my mouth, harder, then down my throat as your hand rests on the back of my head.

"Yeah," you say. "Suck me just like that."

You start to fuck my face, slow and easy, your hips moving in time with my thrusts onto your cock, my easy two-fingered slide into your pussy. You move like a dancer, like the star of some porn-theater ballet, your muscles fluid with every motion. Each time your hips roll, each time I feel the head of your rubber cock slide easily down my throat, each time I feel your cunt clenching around my fingers, my pussy surges, begging for you. I know I'm going to do it—I'm going to risk Jamie's wrath and take you.

But first, I know you're going to come. You've got a G-spot just like other women, and I feel it swollen against my fingertips as I push in, up, out—and as you grasp my hair, pulling it just the way I like it. Your hip motions become less fluid and more intense, your whole body quivering as I feel you ready to let go. And then, in a rush, the thick jet fills my cupped palm and your pussy spasms around my fingers. I don't even know what I'm doing as I slide your cock out of my mouth and dip my face down to drink, catching the pooling streams as you throw your head back and scream, bucking your hips with every jet from your pussy. And after every foul jet of man's come I've tasted, every sour leak of pre-cum, the taste of your juice is almost enough to set me off. I'm ready to come, almost, just from tasting and feeling you, just from looking up at your gorgeous face as you stare down at me in postorgasmic rapture. Your pleasure is nothing at all like a man's—nothing remotely like the furtive, desperate, angry release that spells the end of a twenty-dollar trick.

Softly, I say it: "Will you still fuck me?"

"I thought you said you didn't do full service. You don't have to, now. You got me off good, Eden."

I shake my head. "Please don't go without fucking me. Please?"

You look down at me and shrug.

"You got me off good. You're off the hook. You don't have to fuck me."

And I feel the stab of pain, longing, need that tells me I'm going to be left again, left alone to go back to Jamie.

"You're sure you don't want to? You paid for it and everything."

"Nah," you say. "I'm finished. Keep the fifty."

I nod, my body aching as I struggle to my feet, the desire hurtful in my pussy. I want to climb into your lap and insist that you fuck me, but that's not the way it's done. Instead, I wriggle down my spandex skirt, pull my tube top back on, straighten my clear plastic jacket. You've got your cock tucked away and your pants zipped and belted.

"You're sure you don't want to?" I ask you as you stand.

"Nah," you say, reaching down and grabbing my ass as you kiss me on the cheek. "See you around."

The movie is still going as you leave the preview booth. Some anonymous stud is fucking some anonymous woman on the screen. I sit in the loveseat, feeling the warmth of your ass, feeling the pulse and ache in my pussy, feeling it drip with hunger for your cock. I slip my hand under my skirt and put one finger, then two, inside myself. I start to rub my clit.

The door opens; a bald guy in a corduroy jacket and polyester pants comes in, catches sight of me.

"Oh...I'm sorry, I didn't realize the booth was occupied."

"Wanna date?" I ask him.

He stammers for a few seconds. I cut him off, "Ten dollars," I say.

"For what?"

I slide out of the seat and get down on my knees, bending forward and pulling up my skirt.

"Full service," I tell him, my voice hoarse with the memory of your cock. "Full service."

Thwack!

Lynn A. Powers

Thwack! The leather belt struck.

"You worm! You don't deserve to lick my boot."

"I'm sorry, Mistress Allison," George whined.

"Now, bend over that table."

"I'm doing it," he said urgently.

"Spit on your hand. Now jerk off." Thwack! "Faster, you peon!" Thwack! Thwack!

"I'm coming!"

Thwack! Thwack! Thwack!

"Aaaaaagh." There was a short pause and some heavy breathing. Then George muttered, "You're the best, Mistress Allison."

"Yeah, yeah. I'll talk to you next week, 'George'." I hung up the phone.

Mimi, my cohort in audio pain, peered over the kelly-green cubicle wall to my right. She covered the mouthpiece to her phone and whispered, "Was that Chicken George?"

I nodded. George gave a whole new meaning to "choking the chicken." Every time he called me, he would jerk off into a semithawed oven roaster. I didn't know about it until he exclaimed, "Oh shit!" near the end of one of our calls. George explained that the wet chicken had slipped out of his hand, causing him to accidentally ejaculate onto the floor. You hear the craziest things as a sex phone operator.

"Have you ever asked Chicken George why he jerks off into a chicken?" Mimi whispered.

I frowned. "I never thought to ask."

"Why not?"

"I don't know." I shrugged. "I never ask these guys anything. I guess the less I know, the better."

"I suppose. I just wish I knew about that chicken," Mimi said, returning to her phone call and the hypodermic needle she was injecting into a large dildo—"to get into the right character."

When I first began as a dominatrix sex phone operator, I found it very interesting. I was exciting hundreds of men who ejaculated just from hearing my voice. Then I realized that I was exciting hundreds of men who ejaculated just from hearing my voice. It was never sexually exciting for me. At first it was a power thing. Now it's just boring. The job has become so boring that I've started bringing toys to play with while I work. Today, I brought a slinky that Squeak gave me as a present. I went on to my next caller, droning out my usual routine: "My breasts are huge, they're 40 triple-E...." Joe, our balding, polyester-wearing supervisor, screeched to a halt at my cubicle.

He pointed at the slinky and mouthed angrily, "What the hell is that?"

I covered the mouthpiece of the phone and whispered, "Bondage," while wrapping it around my throat.

Joe winked and gave me a thumbs-up as he walked past to listen to Mimi spin her tales of PVC and snake oil.

OK, if I'm not in it for the excitement of the sex, what am I in it for? It's not a bad job. The hours are flexible and the room is air-conditioned—a major plus in the sweltering New Orleans summer. Besides, I can work my schedule around my lovers' work hours. Squeak is a waitress and works nights. Nathan is a computer geek who works days. Since Squeak isn't into the whole "threesome" thing with a man, I have to arrange my schedule to fit all our needs. Joe lets me do that.

It was closing in on 11 P.M. and the light on my phone was blinking. The last client before my shift ended. I picked it up. "Yeah?"

It was Joe. "New one. Name's Ted. Likes flat-chested red-heads with big hips who will let him suck their strap-on dildo."

"Got it," I said.

I hit the blinking extension and said in a commanding voice, "This is Mistress Allison. Get on your knees and tell me your name."

• • •

After an evening of cock licking, tit fucking, ass rimming, and balling, I was ready for some nice wholesome lesbian sex with Squeak. I quickened my pace through the humid July night just thinking about her perfect white skin. Squeak is the most homosexual person I have ever known. She told me that she tried to have sex with a man once and actually threw up all over him. For that reason, Squeak has never understood my job. Nor does she understand my relationship with Nathan. His presence in my life is made tolerable only by his offerings of cocaine and ecstasy. She has never complained about Nathan—as long as I didn't make love to her the same day I had sex with him. The possibility of touching or tasting his "juices" was too much for her to bear.

I arrived at Squeak's cramped apartment in the French Quarter and let myself in with my key. For a brief moment, I wished I were at Nathan's. After a long day of telling people how to fuck, I wanted to be the submissive. The thought evaporated when I saw Squeak walk out of the bathroom with a towel wrapped around her slim body.

"I was just about to take a shower," she said, scratching her mousy brown crew cut hair. "Wanna join me?"

I threw off my jacket and walked toward her. I placed my hands on her bare shoulders, stroking her smooth skin. I took hold of her towel and pulled it off. Squeak self-consciously wrapped her thin arms around her chest. Gently holding her hands, I pulled them away to see her flat stomach and small, perky breasts. She was gorgeous with her soft, round face, tiny up-turned nose, and pouty lower lip. I bet that most hetero-males pass her by, consider her plain just because she doesn't wear makeup or feminine clothes. Yet I could see the beauty in her. It was understated, though unmistakable.

Squeak playfully pulled away and darted into the bathroom. Then she peeked her head out from the door. "Coming?"

I threw my clothes off as fast as I could, finding Squeak inside the shower, water already flowing around her. I slid open the glass door, stood behind her, and began stroking her breasts.

"Ah!" I jumped back. "The water's hot!"

Squeak turned around and giggled. "Sorry! Let me adjust it."

As Squeak turned to fidget with the knobs, I lathered my hands with the bar soap, then rubbed them around her bottom in a soft, circular motion. I slid the soap between her ass cheeks. Squeak gave a low moan that encouraged me to slide my hands around the front of her thighs and stroke their insides. She leaned back against me as my hands traveled up her smooth, tight belly. My left hand gently caressed her belly ring while my right hand lathered her small breast with the soap. Squeak's head rested against my chest and I bent down to gently nip at her ear. Her hands reached backward and held the outside of my thighs.

I expected Squeak to turn around and reciprocate my touch, but instead she allowed herself to be completely taken away in the moment. I was turned on even more. I lathered Squeak's breasts and softly kissed her neck. She thrust her ass into my legs and arched her back. She muttered something softly, but I couldn't hear her. I stroked her ribs with the soap and then further down beyond her navel. As I lathered her pubic hair, I gently pulled on the small curls, released them, and then gently pulled again. My hand slipped down lower and lathered her labia and clit. I rubbed harder and harder, teasing her. Squeak ground her hips harder into my body, and I rolled her nipple between my thumb and forefinger. I closed my eyes and wished that I had a cock, to penetrate her hard and deliberately. Without warning, I thrust three fingers into her, up to my second set of knuckles, then quickly pulled them out. Squeak inhaled quickly and tried to catch her breath.

I forced her to place her hands against the wall. I brought my hips close to her ass and pretended I was a man as I thrust my three fingers into her again and again. My pelvis mimicked the motion, as if my hand were a cock. My hand slid easily in and out of her. Inside she was wet and warm. Her pussy clamped onto my fingers and I thought I would come just from feeling her excitement. I yanked her left nipple and fucked her as hard as I could. Squeak was making her little squeaking noises, but this time they sounded urgent. It was difficult to keep my balance, so I turned her around and squatted before her. I jammed four fingers into her, as hard and as far as I could. Squeak screamed and desperately pawed the walls. I squatted and brought my lips gently to her clit. I just held my lips there for a moment, tasting the salt. Sucking Squeak's clit, as I would the tiniest cock, made her scream louder and louder. The walls of her cunt held my hand so tight that I could no longer thrust as hard. I tried to ease my entire hand in. I pounded my fist against her labia, slowly yet force-fully. My tongue flicked her clit. I began sucking it harder and harder, keeping with the rhythm of my pounding. Squeak let out one hard scream and her cunt convulsed against my hand. As her vaginal spasms slowed, her body finally relaxed. I pulled my moist hand out from between her thighs and gently kissed her clit, then her pubic hair. I looked up at Squeak. She was breathing hard. She opened her eyes and looked sleepily into mine. Then she dropped to her knees, grabbed my head, and stuck her tongue into my mouth. She pulled hard at my head, and I could feel the teeth of her open mouth press into my lips. Squeak pulled away and hugged me desperately.

"I love you, I love you," she whispered.

I was grateful at her outpouring of love, but a little annoyed that she was now spent. For the past week, Squeak had not once tried to bring me to orgasm. I would now spend the rest of the evening in her arms, comforted yet frustrated.

• • •

"And don't ever call me again, you maggot!" I yelled into the phone. This particular client, "Brad," loved it when I told him never to call me again. He said it made him feel "naughty."

The phone rang as soon as I put it down.

"Mugs?" It was Squeak.

"Hey, Hon," I said, settling back in my chair.

"Listen," Squeak said, "I can't do lunch today."

"What?!"

"I'm sorry," Squeak apologized.

"But it's our anniversary weekend." I could hear my voice getting whiney.

"I know. I'm sorry—I really am."

"What's wrong?" I became concerned. It wasn't like Squeak to cancel a big date like this one.

"Everything is OK," she said quickly. "Something has come up for Saturday. But I can't talk now because I'm at work. I'll explain it later, OK?"

116

"I understand," I nodded into the phone. It was probably family problems. Sometimes her mother breezed into town unexpectedly and laid huge guilt trips on Squeak. I only aggravated the situation by reminding the woman that her daughter was a lesbian. Squeak had said that it was best for her if I kept out of sight.

Squeak asked, "We're still on for brunch Sunday, right?"

"Yeah, Sweetie," I answered. I had spent an entire week's salary on the whole wine-and-roses thing. I decided to surprise her early Saturday morning anyway, before her wretched mother showed up. That would help ease the pain. All of a sudden, I spied Joe. "Uh-oh, gotta get back to the dungeon."

I was disappointed that our plans had changed. Nathan was going to be out of town on business until Sunday, and I wanted to focus my entire attention on Squeak. Saturday would mark one year since we had started going out. I couldn't believe I had dated someone for that long—never mind *two* people.

• • •

Saturday morning I inserted my key into the lock, slowly turning it until I heard the click. I picked up the grocery bags and quietly crept into Squeak's apartment. The shower was running. Perfect! Squeak would never hear me preparing breakfast. I placed the bags on the kitchen counter and immediately altered my plans. The shower was the ultimate place to make love. Maybe this time we could both share in the fun.

I tiptoed to the bathroom and slowly turned the door handle. The door didn't have to open very far for me to see that something was wrong. The woman in the shower was not only taller, but much darker than Squeak. My mouth hung open as I watched this voluptuous black woman lather her hair. I silently pulled the door closed.

I ran into the bedroom—the only room I hadn't entered. No Squeak. Grabbing the grocery bags, I left and sprinted around the block just in case she was walking back from the corner market. I dropped the bags and myself onto someone's front steps. Burying my face in my hands, I tried to figure it all out.

"So *that's* what she had to deal with!" I said out loud angrily.

I know what you're probably thinking, so let me set you straight. I know *I'm* sleeping with someone other than Squeak. But, Squeak, Nathan, and I have an agreement. We have open relationships and can sleep with other people. We just need to tell the others first. It's not simply the disease factor; it's about honesty. Honesty has to be the foundation of any relationship. I should know. All of my previous relationships were broken up because of my infidelities.

"Infidelity!" I yelled at a pigeon. "That's what this is!"

I dumped the grocery bags into a trashcan and stormed back to my apartment. I had to avoid Squeak, so I called Joe and asked for a triple shift. Avoidance is my attempt at anger management. After twenty-four hours, I was sure I would be calm enough to handle the situation.

I was wrong. I became more and more infuriated as the night progressed—much to the pleasure of my clients.

"Oh, Mistress Allison," one client crooned, "I'm going to come."

"Don't you dare!" I screeched into the phone. "You come now and I'll cut it off!"

I don't think the boy could help but have an orgasm. But he was obedient and pretended to wait until I told him to.

"Mugsy!" Joe shouted between calls. "You are hot tonight, girl!"

I peered through my fingers as my head wallowed in misery. Joe was grinning from ear to ear. "Yessirree!" he clapped his hands together. "We've gotten ten callbacks—all people who want to be your regulars." He scratched his head. "I may need to give you an extra shift."

"Yeah, yeah," I muttered despondently. Joe walked away muttering about time schedules and salaries.

My fingers closed in front of my eyes. I knew that I wasn't going to surprise Squeak at 3 A.M., not unless I wanted a surprise like the one I had earlier. Joe was ecstatic when I asked to work Sunday morning.

"Great!" he gleamed, "I'd like for you to work the whole 'football-not-church' crowd."

By the end of my Sunday shift, I was angrier than ever at Squeak. She hadn't called to explain "the situation." I figured the best way to get back at her would be to spend our anniversary dinner with Nathan.

• • •

As I walked over to Nathan's, I started thinking about how selfish Squeak had been this last week. She hadn't brought me to orgasm once. My anger increased as I theorized that this was a result of her preoccupation with her other lover.

Standing in front of Nathan's door, I suddenly realized that my underwear was wet. I was incredibly horny. When you haven't come in a week, almost anything can get you riled up.

I opened Nathan's door with my key and stalked into the room. He was sitting on the couch, white shirtsleeves rolled to the elbow, bent over his laptop computer. I loved looking at Nathan. Even when he was working he looked peaceful. He had an elegant way about him, moving smoothly as though he was at a cocktail party in a 1940s movie. He brushed his jet-black hair away from his face and smiled.

"Mugs!" He moved toward me, folding my body into his. I breathed in his scent and was happy at that moment that there was nothing feminine about him.

Nathan gently kissed my lips. "If you give me a few minutes to finish up, I'll take you out to dinner."

I didn't want to wait until after dinner to get fucked. The urge became immediate and animalistic. I unbuckled his pants and pulled out his semierect cock. As I dropped to my knees, I gently pushed back his foreskin with my lips. My tongue encircled the tip and he became immediately erect.

"Mugs, I've got to finish...." The sentence was completed with moans.

I slid his entire cock into my mouth. I could smell his musky pubic hair. My lips moved back to the tip and I sucked. His cock pushed to the back of my throat as he gently pulled my head toward him. My tongue hungrily rubbed the bottom of his prick. I sucked slowly as I firmly held onto his thighs. The thrusting became faster and I quickly pulled my face away. I had come here to get fucked, not to service.

I stood up and pulled off my sweater. "Fuck me," I purred.

Nathan looked shocked. I never used my "work voice" with him.

We briefly looked at each other and then tore into each other's clothes. A few buttons skittered along the floor as I ripped off Nathan's shirt. The tip of my leather belt gently slapped my back as Nathan yanked it from my jeans. Soon we were on the wood floor, kicking off shoes, pulling socks, tugging at underwear. Nathan didn't stop for foreplay. He threw himself on me, plunging his cock in. I gasped. The momentary pain gave way to frantic pleasure, and I clawed at his back. My eyes rolled up into my head and I closed my lids.

"Fuck me! Fuck me!" I gasped.

Nathan stopped only for a moment. Again, I had used my work voice. He hammered his cock into me even harder. I had never been penetrated so deeply. Loud screams escaped my mouth, and soon Nathan was echoing them. Before I knew it, a powerful orgasm washed over my body. Nathan convulsed; his entire weight collapsed onto me. I held him for a long time, until our hearts calmed back to normal. Nathan kissed me gently and rolled over. My hand brushed the perspiration over the sparse hairs on his chest.

Nathan caught his breath and said, "My God, that was wonderful."

I nodded in agreement.

He turned and smiled. "Now, dinner?"

I slowly put my clothes back on and shook my head. I decided to face the problem head-on. "I have to see Squeak. It's our anniversary."

"Oh, yeah." Nathan grabbed his shirt and assessed the damage. "Hey, what do you want to do for ours?"

I kissed his forehead, grateful he remembered. "We'll talk about it later," I muttered. My mind was already preoccupied with Squeak.

I was now half an hour late to meet her. I gave Nathan one last passionate kiss and left.

I was depressed about Squeak's other woman, but the anger soon returned. My stride changed from a saunter to a march—all the way into Squeak's apartment. She was sitting on her bed reading a magazine.

"There you are," she said with a smile as she closed the magazine. "I was getting worried."

I was stunned. How could she be so sweet when she was cheating on me?

"I called your apartment," she continued, "but you weren't home."

I ground my teeth. She was acting as if nothing was wrong.

"So," she said, giving a little bounce on the bed. "Where are we going to eat?"

I wanted to physically assault her but kept my hands at my side.

"I was thinking...." Her words were drowned out by the wicked thought that crept into my head.

My hands sprung up and onto her tits. I clawed my way through her shirt and tank top and began nipping at her breasts.

"Mugsy!" Squeak was shocked but obviously loved my impulsiveness.

She reached behind me and pulled my shirt up over my head. We were soon naked and I was teasing her by licking her stomach, moving down toward her pussy. When her hips began to writhe, I stopped, rolled over on my back, and commanded, "Eat me out!"

Squeak was motionless. She knew I talked to my customers this way, but never to her.

"Eat me out!" I commanded and added silently in my head, *bitch*. Squeak moved between my legs and cautiously licked my clit.

"Fuck me with your tongue!" I called out sternly.

Squeak hesitated but did as she was told. I was still horny from my escapade with Nathan. I closed my eyes and saw her tongue enter where Nathan's cock had just been. She didn't know it, but she was eating his come. The thought turned me on, and I thrust my hips harder into her cheeks.

I yelled in my mind: *Lap it up! That's what you get for fucking with me!*

I moaned louder and smiled. I felt wicked—I *wanted* this revenge. Soon I was coming just as hard as I did with Nathan. I was so turned on by my little scheme, I could have continued forever. But Squeak was now cuddling up next to me.

"That was weird," she said and kissed my cheek.

"Huh?" I was still smiling.

"I've never seen you so aggressive." Squeak was now stroking my hair.

I patted her thigh and said sarcastically, "Well, after one year, you've got to try something new, right?" I placed my hands behind my head. "Don't want to get bored, do you?"

Squeak shrugged. She kissed me again and gathered my clothes.

"Hey, Mugs," she called over her shoulder. "I'm sorry about lunch and not calling you yesterday. My old college friend Wanda came in from out of town."

I propped my head up. *So, here's the bombshell.* I feigned interest. "Oh, yeah?"

Squeak sat on the chair facing me. "Yeah. She drove in unexpectedly from Baton Rouge on Friday."

"Really?" I said knowingly. I began grinding my teeth. I couldn't believe she would wait for our anniversary to tell me this.

Squeak stopped putting on her shoes. "It was sad, Mugs," she added, looking as if she were about to cry. "Her mother had dropped dead," she snapped her fingers, "just like that. Wanda had no idea she was even sick." Squeak shook her head and continued dressing. "The rest of her family treats her like shit because she got pregnant and married her college professor. Remember? I told you about her."

"Oh, yeah," I said, recalling the faint memory. All of a sudden, I got a queasy feeling in my stomach.

"Anyway," Squeak continued, "I let her crash here so she could avoid all the relatives hanging out after the funeral. She was really upset. We spent all our free time talking about her mom." Squeak stood up and was ready to go. "So, what about dinner?"

Nausea swept over me. "I don't feel so good all of a sudden." I sat up and frantically gathered my clothes.

"What's wrong?" Squeak asked.

"Nothing." I hastily threw on my clothes and grabbed my shoes. "A touch of the bug, I think. It's going around at work. I'll make it up to you, I promise." I zoomed out the door.

I walked home like a zombie. Squeak's words played over and over in my head. Then, the images of my evil deed flashed before my eyes. I was embarrassed that I never once gave Squeak the benefit of the doubt. I felt dirty for using Nathan to get back at Squeak, and doing the one thing Squeak would find unforgivable.

Tears were streaming down my face by the time I was home. I kicked my couch and ranted about how stupid I was. This must have gone on for hours. But at some point, in the early hours of the morning, I began to change my perspective.

"How was I supposed to know?" I yelled at the ceiling. Anyone would have jumped to the same conclusion. Besides, no one knew what I had done, so no one could be hurt. Nathan got great sex, and I spiced up Squeak's sex life a little. None would be the wiser. This secret would go to my grave, and everything would return to normal.

• • •

The next day, I was exhausted from being up all night. I was distracted and knew I couldn't give the kind of performance that I gave over the weekend. Chicken George called, so I decided to have a little fun to take my mind off my troubles.

"Tell me about the chicken, George," I commanded in a throaty voice.

George didn't respond immediately. This was the first time I had ever mentioned the chicken.

I slammed the ruler against my desk. "Don't make me punish you!" I screamed. "Tell me how you do it!"

"I, uh, enter it...."

"Where?" I was getting annoyed. "Which end?" George was always so whiney.

"Well, uh, where the neck used to be." George added meekly, "I hold onto its wings."

George stopped, and I prompted him, "Tell me what it feels like!"

"Uh, it's cold..." he stammered.

"And?" I asked impatiently.

"It's slippery…" he continued.

"Go on!"

I heard George gulp. "It's not completely frozen, you know," he explained. "I like it that way."

"Why?" I roared into the phone.

"Well," George said, gaining a little confidence now. Perhaps he was happy that someone was finally interested in his chicken. "I like it firm, but I like the skin to move. Just a little. Just a little, like this…."

I realized George was getting off on his own description. I propped my feet on the desk. This was going to be an easy call.

George's voice got lower, and he talked rhythmically to the thrusts he was probably foisting into his fowl. "The skin gives a little as I push it back and forth onto my cock. The inside, the inside is, oooh, so cool, and the outside, uh, keeps warming to my touch—yes, and the tip of my cock, oh, can feel its little ribs, and I get harder and harder, yes, the bird, ooh, it swallows me, oh, and I can do it hard! And harder! And harder! And Ugh! Ooh! Ahh!"

I waited a moment for him to compose himself. I asked him quietly. "Why? Why a chicken, George?"

George gasped for air. "Well, you see, I cook the chicken for dinner." He hesitated, but continued. "It's the only way I can get my wife to eat my come."

I dropped the phone, mortified. I was worse than Chicken George. I kicked my chair and walked out of the building.

Hair Club for Bisexuals
Carol Queen

I finally made an appointment to get my hair cut today, at the trendy little salon in my suddenly trendy neighborhood. I have been trying to hold out for long hair, in spite of the fact that I haven't successfully grown long hair since I had it cut off, against my better judgment, in high school. My compromise this time was clipping it up: rhinestone clips if I was up to something fancy or little plastic jaws when just trying to do the librarianesque "You can have me if you take my hair down" kind of thing. Granted, I wasn't making it easy on you—I always wore four or five clips, adding another half-dozen plastic butterflies if I was really playing hard to get. But it's too late for that now. I can't catch the fine hairs, brown in back, going splendidly silver up front at my temples, in a clip anymore. No more showing off my nape, unclasped strands tendrilling down. The kiss spot will just barely be hidden by a demure sweep of hair.

My Hair Girl is way too young to remember firsthand the slick magazine pages I have in mind when I say, "My partner likes it when you cut it Breck Girl." She grins, though; all the hair people, even the ones who weren't born yet, must know about those pastel pictures of women with hair too good to be true, or maybe she's remembering the TV commercials of the seventies. No, I couldn't even pray for hair like that, but maybe she gets it anyway as she lifts the limp wisps away from my face and then leads me to the long communal basin. She leans me back. She's femme, but has a trace of the mistress too: puts my head in the basin's groove, moves me bodily until I'm at the right angle to shampoo. Then, familiarly, she washes my hair, using four times as many sweet, slick hair products as I ever do at home, and her fingertips find tight neck muscles and rub them looser. It's so intimate, yet I'm facing away, and though I know that everyone at this salon gets the same treatment or some variation on it, it still feels as if I'm being taken to a place of great openness. I feel as if I could unclose my eyes and an erotic adventure would have started instead of a haircut.

But she's still dressed when I get up to go to the chair, all the other salon workers and customers too, and I settle in. For some reason I don't open my eyes once during the whole cut and style—no chatting today, just reverie and feeling her hands. She is really quite masterful: moving my head around to suit herself, hands right on my neck and scalp, or else using my hair like fine pony reins, putting me where she wants me. Well, I always like that. It's one of the reasons I want to have long hair, after all: giving my tresses up to a lover so that he or she can grab the reins and ride. I like having my hair pulled—not yanked, usually, but just the way I love it when my limbs are positioned for me and I'm turned into a fuck-doll. I love having my hair treated as if it's there for the taking. In real life it won't grow long or thick enough, it's too fine to really be used to haul me around, but I can dream.

I'm not a hair fetishist, not really. I love Robert's hair as it is now, daddy-short in a flattop, and as it was when it was so long that he, too, wore it all gender-fucky in plastic clips. It was softly curly then. His hair now is animal, especially when wet—some indescribable place between bristly like a hedgehog's and soft like a cat's. But more, I think, like a seal, though I've never touched a live seal so I can't be sure. My first girlfriend had a perfectly straight, thick drape of strawberry blonde hair; it obscured her fingers moving on her guitar's strings, obscured her face as she sang. Another girlfriend had hair so much finer, even, than mine that it was like spun silk, the only remotely femme thing about her; when we drove in her old Peugeot with the sunroof open it would fly crazily skyward as if trying to escape. A halo of gold, an angelic sign on a woman whose hands were always stained with motor oil.

I can't even feel the Hair Girl's hands on my head or in my hair. I feel my head changing positions so I know she must be adjusting me, exposing my nape so that she can snip it bare, side to side, where I can read her deliberation in the slow *sni-i-i-ick* of the scissors. She's delicate, though, precise. I'm sure it's going to be a good haircut. Even the poet William Butler Yeats had a thing for good hair: "Only God, my dear, / Could love you for yourself alone, / and not your yellow hair," he wrote to someone whose tresses inspired not just him, but everyone in the region. A blonde Irish pony that everyone in town wanted to ride.

I'm not a hair fetishist—not really. I've never chosen a lover specifically because of her hair. I've never turned on to a man just because his hair was long, straight, curly, or fuzzy, as we used to sing way back when, when hair was, if anything, even more important than it is today. Although I'm not a hair fetishist, I *can* be impressed. Our girlfriend J's hair was thick and hennaed red, luxuriant and somehow just begging to have hands sunk into it while palms cradled her cheeks. I'm not very toppish in real life, but hair like that—or maybe it was the look in her eyes, which the gorgeous red hair framed—just made me want to fist my hands in it, pull her in, devour her.

The last time we had a date with Jack and Linda, I started marveling at their long hair, each so different—hers dark and sculpted, falling down her back like a smooth waterfall, and his long, light, wild, a silvery cascade.

Linda's not really tall, though she seems that way—the hair adds to her length. Her limbs are slim in my hands, such a good fit, the way it felt the first time I held a woman in my arms, realized sex would have whole new dimensions now that I would sometimes be the same size as my lovers, or even bigger than. Linda's touch is so sure, so practiced, and so cool. She is practiced in her body, too. I know what works for me but don't always ask for it. Sometimes I prefer to take the train ride into the magic tunnel to see what will happen, if the stars are lining up. If they're not, I can always reach down and touch my own clit.

Last time a nirvana moment happened, I was lost under a curtain of Jack's hair, like mosquito netting in a tent in paradise, another place and time. He fucked me into such a perfect arc of taking it, of *I want it,* that somewhere mid-yell the talisman he wore around his neck, which had just been tapping and teasing my nipples before he rose up higher, slipped into my mouth. Suddenly I was fucking it too, lost under that wild sweep of hair.

Of course it had to occur to me, lost that way, that his hair would make perfect pony reins: head thrown back and back arched, rising over him and fucking his ass. For that matter, my partner Robert could fuck him while I watched.

I carefully skirt the notion of using Hair Girl's hair like reins, because I think hair girls and boys, captive audiences as they are, should be the ones to make the first move. So I keep at bay—barely—a cascade of images that might otherwise sweep through me when she pulls my head back again by my hair.

I finally open my eyes. Oh, what a cute haircut, a sleek sweep over my eye, a completely different look than I walked in with. I'm in a rather different mood now, too. My dad, who used to be a barber, would call this "pixie-ish." Are there still pixies? Am I one, even sometimes?

At home Robert says, "Oh, I always want to fuck you when your hair is all Breck Girl."

The Devil Is a Squirrel
Astrid Fox

The devil's not so bad in the sack, you know.

She's not. Not if she tries, anyway. She can get a little lazy, what with her hot 'n' horny reputation and all. But let's face it, things tend to go her way: the filthiest and most satisfying curses, the most delectable transgressions, the moistest chocolate cake—and she's got all the best songs.

I met the devil last August in a grimy, Hell's Kitchen section of East London—my neighborhood, actually. It being London, and also being the wettest English year on record since 1776, it was raining.

I was in a bad mood last August. I had had it with polyfidelity, with monogamy, and particularly with celibacy. As a result of the disastrous consequences of the two former conditions, I had been practicing the latter for a good few years. Six years, six months, and six days, to be precise. By choice, obviously. Obviously, by choice. I had made a conscious decision to value my sexual self and change my non-sexual-self-respecting life by making different conclusions the next time around. So obviously, it was by choice.

It always is, right? *Right?* So stop snickering. I hadn't been laid since February 9th, 1994. Last summer, the middle of postmillennial August should have been a swelteringly hot, steamy, sunny day, yet I was drenched in the middle of Hackney. I was miserably soaked. Miserably soaked and shagless is a terrible condition to be in. I had gotten way past any concept of blue balls, or blue labia, many years before.

I was having a dry spell in the middle of England's wettest spell ever. There was irony in there somewhere, but by that point I was far too bitter to care.

I was taking a shortcut home, my jacket pulled up over my head, since I had lost my umbrella on the underground on the way in to work. I was mumbling something about the cursed, bloody weather and cursed, bloody fellow pedestrians who insisted on walking where I wanted to walk and cursed, bloody cars splashing through cursed, bloody puddles; mumbling how the devil could take them all, because I'd had it. I'd absolutely had it: with life, with London, with my perpetual paucity of shags, and I'd be damned if I was going to spend yet another year with a big fat zero on the action front.

I dodged the traffic at last and cut through an alley, trying to remember, with some irritation, whether I had anything in the freezer to pop into the microwave for dinner.

And that's when someone hissed at me from the deepest corner of the alley.

"Psst! Come in here!"

Without my umbrella, rain was dripping down my neck. The alley had the semblance of shelter, thanks to a green plastic awning overhead.

"Just a little closer."

I could barely see. I took a moment to wipe the rain out of my eyes and began to make her out more clearly. She appeared to be unarmed. She also looked out of place in the gritty dinge of a trash-covered alley. I say "she" casually, as if the devil was any other female. Let me tell you, she wasn't. Long, sleek dark hair. It looked liquid: like molasses, like treacle, like honey poisoned with ink. She had a knock-out body, too—even asexual little ol' me could see that. Curve to curve to curve. Like a glam-o-rama starlet: really stacked. Said curves were swathed in what looked to be a strapless taffeta frock, circa 1959. It was blue as a prom queen's eyes, but in this dress the dark-eyed woman put all predictable prom queens to shame. Dark hair, sinful eyes, and a to-die-for body in a killer dress. Murder by numbers. (But, see, I hadn't clocked onto the fact that she was the devil yet, you know?)

She smiled at me.

Even then, not knowing what she was, I wanted her to have some effect on me. I wanted her to make my pussy wet and my clit hard, but she didn't. Female impotence is a very weird thing.

"Come a little closer," she requested.

Listen, I didn't want to get stabbed. I stayed where I was.

"Suit yourself." She lit a cigarette. She stared at me. "Well?"

"What do you mean, 'well'?"

"Hey, lady, you're the one who called me up. Now why don't you cut the crap so we can get started?"

"Excuse me?" I was staring with horrified fascination at her as she took exactly three steps toward me. Her hips swayed provocatively. Her cleavage shifted appreciably. Just watching her made my mouth dry, the way you feel when you're watching an especially good theatrical performance. But it didn't make me wet. In fact, it made me annoyed, because when she sashayed up to me and stuck her tits in my face, she blew a purposeful mist of cigarette smoke straight into my eyes.

Her eyes were narrow and glittering. There was a flush to her sallow skin, as if she were particularly excited about something.

I thought about taking a step back. There was only one advantage to staying here in the alley, and that was the fact that it was shielded in part from the rain. The disadvantage, of course, was a possibly imminent mugging.

She didn't move away. "I don't have a lot of spare time, sister. What's it going to be?" She pushed her breasts against my own—quite brazenly, I have to say.

I knew it was a proposition, but I hadn't had one in so long—well, at least not one from anyone who wasn't four sheets to the wind—that I have to tell you, I was a little shocked.

I asked myself what she saw in me: cranky-looking woman of about 40, short hair, glasses, fairly butch (but looked like I could swing for the home team, too, in a rough-and-rugged kind of way). I didn't look straight, gay, *or* bi. I was a female eunuch. More than anything else, I looked grumpy, which I was.

Maybe she was drunk, after all.

"Hey!" She snapped her fingers near my ear, something that always pisses me off. "I mean it. Make your choice: chicks, dicks, combinations thereof, or the red-hot mama herself, yours truly, *au naturel*."

I tried to regain some composure, and cleared my throat. "And who might 'yours truly' be?"

At last she took a step back, and then burst out laughing. "You're great!" she said, not very nicely. "You really don't get it, do you?"

"I'm afraid I don't. Thanks for the invitation, but I'm just going to make my way home, put my frozen dinner in my microwave, settle down, and...."

"Shut up, yeah? Take a look at me. Come on, take a good look." She stood back and did a twirl before posing, rather sarcastically, with her hand on her hip.

I sighed. And then reckoned that the sooner I humored her, the sooner I'd be on my way. So I took a good look this time.

OK, to be fair, she had a hell of an aura, what with that snug dress and her dark hair tossed back as if she was Jessica-fucking-Rabbit. It was a sinister aura. In fact, you could say she glowed with malice and ill intent. If I had been the susceptible type, I might even have called it allure. Her smirk, her blood-dark nail polish, her lush wicked body—it was as if the air around her was sizzling and cackling. I thought of what she said about me "calling her up." I thought back to my cavalier cursing at the London weather and my current nun-like state—the six years, six months, and six days since last I shagged. I wasn't a specialist in the proper cataloging of medieval court records and witch trials for nothing. I got it.

I wasn't particularly shocked. Just as my senses were dulled to sensual pleasure, I was also impervious to full-scale, supernatural shock. After so long without any sort of stimulation, carnal or otherwise, I was kind of floating along in a celibately grumpy haze. Nothing really got to me anymore. Not even this.

"Thanks, but no thanks," I said. "I'm sure you're perfectly delightful, but historically I think there's a downside to playing with fire, if I remember correctly. Loss of one's eternal soul and all that?" My voice trailed off. I was staring at her cleavage, her tits being thrust up by some invisible but terribly effective support system. There was a sheen to her skin. I didn't think it was rain, but just the faintest layer of perspiration. I wondered how hot her skin was on this cold rainy day. I watched a tiny drop of sweat trickle down between her breasts. For the first time in many years, I felt a dim jolt of desire, a little twinge between my legs.

I cleared my throat hurriedly.

"Anyway," I continued awkwardly, "I have to get home."

I found that I was still staring at her tits.

She moved in on me so that she was within a couple of inches, once again. Let me just say this: She was very quick to take advantage of any weakness.

"If you don't mind my saying so," she said in an irritatingly sultry voice, "despite the weather, you look a little dry."

"Excuse me?"

"A little dried up. Like a prune. Am I right? OK, you're no spinster, but let's just say it's fairly evident you haven't had it for a while."

"I beg your pardon?"

"A good long while, I'd say, actually. You're aching for it, aren't you? I bet it feels a lot longer than six and a half years." She abruptly changed the subject. "What's your line of work?"

"I'm a librarian."

"A *librarian?* Please. No surprises there."

"You should talk—look at the color you're wearing. Talk about predictable. How about a little subtlety?"

"How about a little appreciation?"

In a suddenly crude motion, she hiked up her hem and stuck her fingers between her legs. I couldn't see exactly what she was doing, but it was such a vulgar act that a kick of desire jumpstarted in my cunt. The feeling tightened and got worse. She withdrew her left hand with an audibly slurpy sound and raised her fingers to her mouth, smelling them and then slowly licking the juices off them, like the cheapest tart in town.

Her more discreet machinations hadn't worked, but this obscene little display had my clit buzzing as if her tongue was already working at it. It was downright embarrassing. She'd worked out exactly what would get me going, and then did it. I felt uncomfortable. I didn't want to be played like a fucking piano. But now I was horny. Her dark, crimson, full lips made me wonder what her pussy lips looked like; I found myself straining my neck to get a look at the shape of her ass with its plump, high cheeks. Jesus, I felt as if I was melting in her heat already. I almost didn't care.

I closed my eyes for a second, trembling, trying to get a grip on my sanity. It was highly unlikely that I was standing in an alley being propositioned by the devil herself. Maybe lack of nooky had finally driven me round the bend. Maybe one of those cars that had been skidding around on the wet pavement had crashed into me and killed me, and now I was in—heaven? hell? who knew?! I screwed my eyes tightly shut, trying desperately to think. I'd open them, and everything would be fine. I'd open them and I'd be alone in the alley, and then I'd go back to my safe, celibate life.

"Maybe girls aren't your thing? I'm flexible, you know." Her voice was very low and very sultry. I snapped my eyes open.

The bitch was really fucking with my head now. It was becoming harder and harder to convince myself I was sane. Because Temptress No. 1 had disappeared and Tempter No. 2 was in fine form. I don't fuck men all that often—well, up to six and a half years ago I didn't fuck men all that often—but in the good old days I was always open to suggestions.

A certain type of tall, academic, smooth-faced, shy, cerebral boy could always make me go weak at the knees. One with disconcertingly sleazy eyes behind his specs that would belie his mild-mannered appearance. Eyes that made me wonder what perverse thoughts he entertained during the long hours spent studying in the university library. A few of those boys had passed through my own doors of knowledge in the past.

The young man smiling down at me in the alley had exactly that look.

He was smiling, just as she had been, but he didn't have her smirk—his lips were curving politely; unlike her, he seemed passive, waiting for my move. He reminded me just a tad of my first boyfriend, Owen, from when I was fifteen. The biggest difference being that I had known Owen in the seventies and Tempter No. 2 was obviously from our present decade. He had long blond hair tied back in a ponytail and was wearing a scuzzy black heavy-metal T-shirt—reading "Queens of the Paleolithic" (or something like that; I don't keep up much with modern music)—and a pair of loose blue corduroy pants. Blue was a constant theme.

He was observing me carefully, respectfully. He still reminded me of Owen, and suddenly I had a flashback—Owen and me making out until I was as wet as the weather today. My crotch soaked through my tight faded jeans, his hand tensed on a nipple beneath my halter top, his teenage hard-on thick and rock hard beneath his flaring pants, the obligatory plastic comb squeezed in tight against his young ass.

I could nearly smell Owen now, could remember the taste of his mouth and the way his kisses made my heart beat fast. The way I would stroke him until he groaned and came in my fist. The way his hand would glisten, sticky from finger-fucking me in the back seat of my parents' car. Then how we'd kiss again, after everything sweet had happened. Everything was always easy, smooth and sexy, smooth as butter, smooth as cream, smooth as fucking itself, and we'd start all over again.

The devil's eyes were clever and knowing. The devil was as innocent as my very first fuck. The devil knew that, deep inside my celibate, asexual skull, I could still remember things like that. I could still remember sex. And yet this devil was presenting me with an older version of Owen, maybe a university, twenty-something version, not innocent anymore but still eager, young but aware.

He'd learned a few things. There'd been a few Mrs. Robinsons around to instruct him. He was partial to older women, maybe. Maybe he even fancied grumpy old me. The devil knew damn well what he was doing. He pulled me toward him and we kissed. His tongue slid in my mouth quick and tight, tasting of cheap cigarettes and micro-brewed beer, like a college student's tongue should taste. I clung to him. I could feel the heavy push of his cock against my abdomen. I wanted to squeeze my pussy down on him, soft, wet and hot, and just rock and rock.

No! I swung myself away from him, breathless this time. The submission wasn't worth it: a shag for a soul. I don't think so, buddy. No matter how cute and pretty you are, or how many times you'll whisper Chaucer in my ear in the late mornings when you're prone to skipping class.

"You're a hard nut to crack," the devil observed. This time his eyes were neither slow nor sweet. He gave me a once-over with that sleazy gaze, and I remembered all those late-twenty-something Ph.D. boys whom I observed so impassively week after week in my library.

Had I secretly wanted to fuck them all along, and just been unaware of it? Was the devil giving me the kind of man who would finger my asshole on a public bus, daring me to let on to the folks in the seats up ahead? Would he bind my wrists up and just fuck me, use me like a hole, while he selfishly pumped his cock into my soft, sticky center until he, and not I, had enough?

Would I beg him to slap me, and then watch his expression when I whimpered down on my knees? Whimpered in lust mixed with shame and a twist of pain, wondering if maybe he enjoyed the crack on my cheek a little too much?

I was doing it again. The devil was toying with me. He, she, whoever—it wasn't going to get me. The devil might know me inside out, but there was still free choice. My clit was as hard as Owen's teenage cock had ever been. My cunt was wet with desire. When I closed my eyes, I saw the devil's figure: a being with marvelous, luscious tits that were flushed with want. Fantastic tits, with stiff thick nipples of candy-red; tits that made my clit quiver just at the thought; and beneath those breasts a smooth abdomen, and beneath the abdomen a thick long cock already glittering with wetness, as if it had just been withdrawn from a sopping pussy.

The devil had it all. I had to resist.

"I'm sorry," I whispered, "but no."

The devil sounded ever so faintly amused. "There's not a lot of options left, you know. Still, if you insist."

Suddenly, instead of a grungy postgraduate student standing before me, there was a fluffy, bushy-tailed squirrel with bright black eyes. Its tail, I noticed, was blue. It looked like an exotic form of feather duster. Thankfully, the squirrel caused my desire to drain swiftly away. I was going to be all right.

I was going to be in control.

"I don't know where you get your information from," I told the small rodent, feeling pretty stupid about it, too, "but animals really aren't my thing."

"I know," said the squirrel in a midrange voice—wait: said the squirrel! Now I knew things were dire—"I just wanted to illustrate an old German dialectal saying."

"And what's that? 'Don't go down trees head first'?" I asked. I was starting to feel like myself again, though lust was still resonating in little twinges throughout my body.

" 'The devil is a squirrel,' yeah? That's the saying I'm referring to. It means that odd things show up where you least expect them. I personally feel—and granted, I'm biased—that the trick is to take advantage of odd opportunities whenever you can." The squirrel's intonation rose on the last word, and the original dark-haired woman was standing before me, smoothing down her blue dress rather demurely.

It was good that she was human, but of course that meant that desire left me dry-mouthed and shaking all over again. All I wanted to do was fuck her. It was as if all the stored-up, unacted-on desires of the last six and a half years hit me all at once and all I could think of was fucking and all I could see was fucking and all I wanted to do was to start fucking.

It would be worth the price.

A good fuck would always be worth the price of an eternal soul.

For a second I hesitated. I had the weird feeling that there was a struggle going on over my head, perhaps between a tiny demon and a tiny angel hovering above each of my shoulders, as in a Donald Duck cartoon. Maybe it wasn't a struggle. Maybe it was a negotiation. Maybe I didn't give a rat's ass.

"Oh, hang it all." And at last I stepped toward her.

So I fucked the devil. Or rather, she fucked me: three fingers up my wet cunt, with me bent over at the waist, nearly kissing the ground, my sensible librarian trousers bunched around my ankles. Her fingers were as gentle as ramming rods, as tender as a butcher's. These fingers of hers were red-hot pokers sliding into my slit—they would have felt bad, except they felt so good that I just gritted my teeth, tightened my cunt round her rough, hot hand, and came like a house afire. I mean, speak of the devil.

I fucked her as a boy. His mouth sucking and licking my pussy with his finger slyly intruding my asshole. His face shiny with my juice, until I pushed him on his back and rode him. His cock was thick and stiff inside me, and his smooth, scholarly ass rasped against the alley pavement, a nice counterpoint to the rain sparkling in his lashes. His hand tickled out a climax from my clit until the sensation was heavy, intense, crude. Until I would have sold my soul if I were forced to hold out any longer. Until I came, actually.

And I fucked her as a very tasty hermaphrodite: lips round the devil's cock, hand up the devil's snatch. Lovely.

I also fucked the devil in her previously referred to *au naturel* shape, and no, I'm not telling you what that was. I will say, though, that it made my head spin, literally. Have you ever seen *The Exorcist?*

Still, all in all, the devil's an innately selfish person, so toward the end of that wet summer day she got a little lazy. Even that didn't stop me from enjoying every second—a soul's only a soul, after all. It's much better to have fun while you can. I haven't seen her since that occasion. I have spent the ensuing days since last August seducing and being seduced by mere mortals, and now I have to wonder why I ever stopped.

But even though that was last summer, today I realized something rather interesting. I have one over on the devil—a technicality, really: *I'd be damned if I was going to spend yet another year with a big fat zero on the action front*—you see, the fine print, the wording. The thing was, I wasn't damned, because I did get shagged, thanks to the devil. Credit given where credit is due.

I figure she knew this. The devil's pretty experienced when it comes to contractual agreements. So why'd she do it? Was it a pity fuck? Did the devil have a sentimental turn of heart on the 15th of August, 2000? It was a holy day of obligation, after all.

Who knows? Weird things can happen. Fish can fly. Once in a blue moon, and all that.

The devil is a squirrel, yeah?

Leaving the Past
Nine Declare

I wasn't in the mood to meet anyone. I only went out because my friends pestered me, but poky little gay clubs with bad disco music aren't really my thing. I didn't want to stay in on a Friday night. It made me feel as if I had no life. So I thought maybe I'd compromise, go out for just a drink or two, then go home and resume feeling sorry for myself.

I'd had a long week. I'd been working like a dog and getting no recognition for it. I'd had no time to cook, and my flatmates constantly left the kitchen a mess. I'd come home lacking the energy to even wash a dish, so I'd been living on greasy Chinese food from the takeaway downstairs for the past several days. Around 11 o'clock each night I would suddenly feel inspired to stay up and read, or do some writing, or even just watch a film, and then I'd have to get up at 7:30 the next morning. I felt burned out.

To top it all, two of my ex-lovers whom I hadn't heard from in ages both decided to contact me that week. Charlotte gave me a call to invite me to her wedding. I had purposely avoided her since the day I overheard her telling a mutual friend that I was boring in bed. I'd managed to successfully stay out of her way for over two years at this point, and attending her wedding certainly wouldn't benefit that strategy.

And Chris sent me an e-mail—Chris, far away in New England, where he'd been living in the back of my mind for so long now, silent and therefore pain free. And now, finally, a message from him. Just seeing his name in my in-box brought back memories that I couldn't bear. We hadn't been in contact at all since the horrible transatlantic breakup. I couldn't open it. Instead I let it sit there, bothering me all week.

Whenever I caught myself wondering what he had to say, I would remind myself of the things I had to be getting on with this week. I knew that regardless of his message's content, just reading his words would turn me into a wreck. Carrying on with these rationalizations, I still hadn't managed to end the suspense, and was now starting to wonder what was worse, because that unopened e-mail gnawed at me every time I logged on.

So there I was, at this club, with a bunch of friends who were all in high spirits, and me, gripping my alcopop as if my life depended on it. I was trying not to be pensive and miserable, thinking if this was only a proper, quality gay club then I could go sit down at a table and an e-headed pretty boy would be there to give me a shoulder massage. But no. This place wasn't my sort of thing, dingy and smoky, full of old men and bouncers who grilled me at the door because my hair was longer than an inch, and—you've been to Edinburgh, haven't you? OK, then you know the place I'm talking about.

I stood by the side watching my friends dance and whoop it up. There was no way I felt like dancing. It didn't really matter, because I don't dance much anyway. Hector stood next to me and kept me supplied with nasty French cigarettes.

"So what's wrong with you?" he finally asked after I'd tried my best to make convincing small talk.

"Oh, nothing. I'm just in a crappy mood. Sorry I'm not great company." I exhaled and stared at the butch dyke vogueing in the mirror. Hector rolled his eyes.

"What you need is to get laid," he confided.

"Yeah, right." I never got laid these days. I suppose I never did much in the first place, which could perhaps explain my unimaginative way of navigating things with Charlotte. And right now, I was off people for Lent. It seemed best to take a break from my string of shattered relationships.

"It's not going to happen," I said simply. "Especially not here," I added as an afterthought.

"What? Don't you see anyone you like?" He sounded surprised, so I squinted through the smoke and flailing limbs. I counted several dozen gay boys—some were cute, but not going to be attracted to me by any stretch of the imagination—and just a few women. One or two were probably straight, which left me with a couple of butch dykes. It wasn't that I found them unattractive, but I'd seen them around a lot, and had never really connected.

I shrugged half-heartedly.

"Anyway," I said after a beat, "tell me about *you*. Who are you shagging at the moment?"

"Hector!" He was about to answer me when Daniel, who had left the dance floor, jumped on him, distracting his attention. "I'll get this round," breathed Daniel.

"God, you're all sweaty." Hector ruffled his hair. "Gross."

Daniel stuck his tongue out and headed off to the bar. As an afterthought he stopped and returned. "What're you having?" he asked me.

"Oh. Um. Something vodka-related. Surprise me. Thanks."

"That's who I'm shagging," said Hector conspiratorially once Daniel was out of earshot.

"Very nice." I'd only met Daniel a couple of times but he seemed OK. "Anyone else?"

"Yeah, but he doesn't know." I looked at Hector sternly, and he waved away my disapproval. "Don't even start," he said, blowing a smoke ring in my direction.

"Whatever." I wasn't in the mood to debate morals. Daniel returned clinging to three bottles, with a tall woman in tow.

"Look who I found!" he exclaimed cheerily.

"Lisa!" Hector was all smiles. The smoke cleared a little and I saw Lisa properly. She had shoulder-length, bleached blond hair, a gorgeous smile, brown eyes, and an un-made-up face; she was wearing a sexy little black top that showed off her fine cleavage, and khaki combat trousers. "Lisa's from Glasgow," Hector explained to me. "She's an old friend of Dan's." He turned back to her. "What are you doing across here, babes?"

"I had a job interview today," she said. Her voice was low and sounded a little smoky, which I have always found attractive. "I thought I'd stick around until the last bus and see if anyone I knew was here. Hi, I don't think we've met. I'm Lisa." She extended a hand toward me.

"Terra. Nice to meet you." I tried to behave like a normal human being, but my brain was making fire engine noises. Gorgeous woman! Gorgeous woman! Who'd have thought I would actually meet one here?

"Terra? That's an unusual name. It's nice, I like it." She smiled at me and I tried not to melt.

"Tell us about the interview," Hector instructed, taking out his cigarettes again and offering them round.

"It's an advertising thing. To be honest, I don't know if I could stand it, but I want to move back here, and going on interviews never hurts."

"Well, good luck," said Daniel. "It would be good to see you more often. Lisa's brilliant," he said to me. "Really wicked." I nodded appreciatively, tongue-tied.

"Terra here is a web consultant," announced Hector. "Aren't you, Terra?" Lisa raised her eyebrows as if she was interested.

"A soon to be out of work web consultant," I muttered darkly. "I'm afraid I'm about to get a permanent holiday." I wished I hadn't complained, as soon as I'd said it. I was sounding miserable again. Hector offered something glib by way of a response, but Lisa excused herself to use the ladies' room. Daniel disappeared back onto the dance floor after giving Hector a quick peck.

"Really, Terra," Hector scolded. "You're not going to pull if you're so negative all the time."

"I know, I know. But who even said that I wanted to pull?"

"Oh, you're not fooling anyone. She's divine. Even I can appreciate that, and I'm as gay as a goose." He blew a smoke ring. "You'll like her. A lot."

"Well, it doesn't matter. I don't even know how to talk to women. I don't know what to do. So it's kind of a foregone conclusion."

"Oh, listen to Miss Misery-guts!" Hector settled himself against the wall and took a swig from his beer. "You'll never get anywhere if you keep thinking along those lines. That's the first rule. And the second is, just be yourself."

I smiled wryly. Lisa returned from the toilet and smiled at us both. "How do you know Dan and Hector?" she asked me.

"Well, I know Hector better. We've known each other for a couple of years."

Hector draped an arm around my shoulder. "Tell her how we met, babe."

I groaned and shook my head—convinced Lisa wouldn't want to hear our stupid story. But Hector poked me in the rib and glared.

"OK, so a friend of mine had just bought a scooter, and I decided to steal it. I was tearing down the street with him running after me, scaring all the pedestrians, and then I crashed into this one here." Hector laughed, as he did every time he made me tell this story. He prodded me again to continue.

"Hector fancied my friend, so he took us out for drinks and ended up shagging Marty that night. I was crashing at Marty's, so I was on the sofa in the next room and had to listen to all of it. The next day when Marty went to work Hector took me out for brunch to compensate for my trauma. So that's how we got to know each other."

"That's pretty cool," said Lisa. "Hey—is that the Marty who works in Jenner's?"

"He used to, yeah."

"He's the one who shagged my mother's boyfriend, in that case."

"Whoa," we all agreed.

"Small world."

Cher's "Love After Love" came on at this point, and Hector got up to go dance with the rest of the boys. He winked at me as he left the two of us alone.

I stood there for a moment unable to think of anything to say. I was trying not to look at Lisa's cleavage, which was fantastic.

"I like your clothes," I blurted out after what felt like an uncomfortable amount of time had passed.

"Oh, do you? Thanks. I think they might have been inappropriate for a job interview."

"You never know, I guess."

"Everyone there was wearing black suits. It was horrible. And the women were all wearing impossibly high heels." I looked down at her boot-clad feet.

"I can't do heels either," I confided. "Never even tried."

"Yeah, fuck that," she agreed. She lifted her bottle to her lips, keeping her eyes trained on me. "So tell me something about yourself, Terra." She drank from it.

"Um." *Be interesting, be interesting.* "Well, I work with computers, as you know. I like to travel, and swim, and read crime novels. I have two cats, and, uh, I can juggle." I can't really juggle. I just added that so that she'd stay awake.

"Really?" Obviously, it worked.

"OK, so tell me something about *you*," I said, before she could ask me to demonstrate.

"I'm looking to move back to Edinburgh now. I met Tina Turner once when I was fourteen. I have many secrets, mostly other people's. I like sunsets and smoking and Truman Capote and whipped cream." I didn't really know what I should say in return, I just sat there with a smile frozen on my face. She laughed and took my hand. "Come on, let's get some more drinks."

So we did. We didn't bother returning to watch the boys on the dance floor; we sat up on bar stools and talked about this and that. She told me some interesting things she'd done, and I told her some semi-interesting things I'd done, and then we started doing shots. After a while we ran out of cigarettes and started asking complete strangers to donate them, grading them on their responses. A bald man glared at us and pretended that he'd never heard us, but most people were friendly, or if they weren't friendly they at least reached into their pockets and handed us smokes in silence.

"You're pretty cute, Terra," she said to me finally. It was 1 o'clock. I had meant to go home and sleep hours ago.

"Thanks. You're not so bad yourself."

She smiled. Then she leaned over and kissed me. She smelled of smoke and Acqua di Gio for men. Her studded tongue explored the inside of my mouth. I reached out and held her by her shoulders, touching the straps of that little black top, wondering if I would get her out of it tonight. Her hands crept up my legs. *No, don't tease me right here,* I thought, *I'm too turned on.* I sighed and continued to kiss her while she deliberately traced a slow line up to the top of each leg, over my old, paint-splattered jeans. Her touch felt electric.

My eyes were closed and I was lost in my own world. I felt her hands on my body and her lips on mine while my brain received random, abrupt images of nothing that mattered.

I saw a space shuttle, then a sign I'd seen on the bus that day that advertised a driving school, then a kid I'd known as a child who had pet turtles, then Pokémon. In the background I heard disco music and the noise of the bar; in the foreground there was her heavy breath and occasional sounds from our kissing.

"Girls, girls, girls!" Hector and Daniel jumped on us. I pulled away.

"We're going home now," Hector said. "Maybe you should too?" He reached out and gave me a friendly punch on the arm. "It was nice seeing you again, Lisa. You girls have a fun night." He kissed each of us on both cheeks.

And they were off.

Lisa looked at me.

"Well," she said. "Do you want to come back to my place? It's in Glasgow, though."

"I live just around the corner, if you'd—"

"Great!" She jumped off the bar stool. "I'll get my coat."

On our way out of the club she suddenly turned and pounced on me. I was pinned to the wall in a secluded corner as she kissed me hard, pressing her body against mine. I reached out to hold her, but she grabbed both my wrists, holding them in one hand at my side. Her other hand traced my shoulder, then worked its way down my left breast, which she squeezed and groped.

She was kissing me hard. I realized I was holding my breath. Her hand worked its way under my shirt, under the cup of my bra, then seemed to think better of it. Lisa drew her face an inch from mine and looked down at my button-up shirt. She undid the top button, then the one underneath, and finally the one below that.

"Not here!" I whispered.

"Shhh," she purred, still holding my wrists together, not hurting but enough to let me know I wouldn't escape without her permission. "No one will see, I promise." She bent her head to my breast, pulling down the bra cup. Her free hand had found my ass. She dug her nails into my buttocks as she sucked on my nipple. I writhed, turned on from what she was doing and from being exposed in public.

I leaned back against the wall. All I saw was her head as her tongue licked its way across my chest to the other nipple, circling it again and again before her lips took over once more. Her hand moved to the crotch of my jeans. Her fingers were slowly massaging me. I let out an involuntary gasp.

Someone walked past us, so close I could hear the footsteps. I stopped responding for a moment, paranoid. She pulled away from my breast and let go of me.

"Right, let's go," she said, almost businesslike.

As I buttoned my shirt and followed her out, I caught sight of the security camera pointed at us. I grinned at it.

We held hands all the way back to my flat, but we didn't speak. I unlocked the door in silence and showed her in. We each removed our shoes at the door, something I always do. She ditched her coat and bag on my sofa, watched as my cat darted out of the room, and looked at me.

"Um. Do you want a coffee, or—?"

She shook her head, standing in the center of the living room, smiling at me. "Which room is your bedroom?" I led her in, closing the door behind us.

Lisa embraced me. "You're very sexy," she said quietly. Her lips brushed against the corner of my eye. "I don't know if you're aware of that." She held me by the waist. I couldn't speak; the silence was deafening and I didn't dare breathe. The next thing she said was barely audible. "I don't know if I'm what you were looking for tonight."

That wasn't something I had expected to hear. For a moment I was too taken aback to answer, then I blurted out, "But I've wanted you from the moment I saw you!"

Lisa looked straight into my eyes for a long moment, looking a little uncertain. Then her confident smile returned. "OK," she said, still smiling at me. "OK."

I didn't know why she would need reassurance, but I pressed myself close to her and kissed her for several long minutes. With both hands I gently eased her black top up over her head. Her small, pert breasts were bare and in perfect proportion to her lithe body. To the right of her navel was a capital *R* in gothic script.

"What does that stand for?" I asked.

"Shhh." Her fingers caressed my lips. "I'll tell you later." I was distracted by her half-naked body and sat down on the bed while she stood before me; I dipped my head between her breasts, sucking and kneading them gently. Lisa leaned her head back and moaned.

"That feels beautiful."

With one hand I traced my nails up and down her naked back; with the other, I gripped her waist, keeping her in place. She shuddered as I scratched her particularly hard, and I stopped for a moment, worried that I'd hurt her.

"No. Don't stop."

I kept on scratching as I gradually worked my way down from her perfect breasts to kiss her tattoo, then lick slowly all the way up her cleavage to her neck. I tugged gently at the side of her neck with my teeth, provoking another blissful moan. Now was the time. My tongue trailed down her body and my fingers reached out to undo the fly button of her combat trousers. It was then that I noticed a bulge. Tentatively I stroked it through the fabric. I felt it swell a little more at my touch.

I looked up at Lisa. She was looking straight down at me, obviously worried about my reaction.

Well, yes, I was surprised. It's not what one would normally expect to find at this point. And I wasn't sure exactly what would happen now, what she would want to do. But I had already decided that a night with Lisa could only be a good thing.

My face broke into a broad smile. I couldn't stop beaming. After a moment Lisa smiled back.

"You're still what I'm looking for," I told her.

With that she regained her confidence. She bent down and pushed me backward so that I was lying on the bed. Crawling on top of me, she kissed me hard, pinning my arms to my sides as she undid the buttons on my shirt with her teeth. The woman had skill! She removed my bra. Her hair trailed across my skin as she sucked my nipples. She released my hands, but I lay there unable to move for a moment, giving her just enough time to unzip my jeans and wrest them off along with my socks.

Now I was only wearing my underwear. I was a little nervous but my clit was throbbing so much, I wasn't going to dwell on any hang-ups. Lisa moved my legs apart so that she could lie on top of me. I could feel her thrusting against me as she continued kissing me deeply. Her tongue stud clicked against my teeth. Her breath was heavy. I held her tightly by the shoulders and moved with her. I could feel how hard she was for me. My panties were soaked.

Lisa grabbed me by the hair, forcing me to keep my head down on the bed. With her other hand she played with my right nipple.

"Do you want to?" she said in a low voice.

I nodded. "Yes."

She peeled my underwear off, and I reached out to finally unbutton those combats. She was wearing plain black panties, which I removed, finally revealing her thick cock. It stirred at my touch. I reached across to my bedside table to get a condom out of the drawer and put it on her.

We kissed for a long time, kneeling on the bed naked, her cock rubbing against my thigh. I lay down again and pulled

Lisa back on top of me. She bit my ear lobe gently and pressed her breasts to mine. I parted my legs and suddenly she was inside me. We were rocking, slowly at first and then faster, faster. I buried my head in her neck and covered her shoulder with bite marks as she writhed and tried to avoid my teeth.

"Sorry," I said.

Lisa shook her head and with one hand grabbed me by the hair again, keeping me in my place. Her other hand encircled my neck. My eyes widened as she gently but firmly held me down by my throat.

"Shhh," she whispered, smiling. She started to thrust harder and I could feel her move deeper inside me. I relaxed as much as I could, allowed her to manipulate me, stared up into her face as she watched my own. Finally she released me, moving her attention to my breasts, which she gripped as she rode me. I returned my hands to her own breasts and pinched her nipples as she moaned.

Opening my legs wider to better accommodate her, I reached up to pull her hair so that she would lower her lips again to mine. I scratched her back again and she thrust harder in return. All that could be heard were the involuntary guttural sounds we made as we focused on thrusting even harder. The bed was rocking and the headboard banged against the wall. Lisa grabbed my breasts so roughly it hurt—in a good way.

The bed slammed harder and louder. Now I was gasping for breath, with Lisa's cock plunging into me. I dug my nails deep into her skin and heard her swear. I came suddenly, panting and exhausted. She collapsed beside me a moment later.

We lay there on top of the tangled bed sheets for a moment, trying to get our breath back to normal. I was sure I was glowing.

After a few minutes Lisa reached out and took my hand.

"It stands for Richard," she told me. I squeezed her hand and raised it to my lips to kiss it.

We gradually crawled under the covers and slept, holding one another. In the morning, after breakfast in bed, we exchanged numbers and she headed back to Glasgow.

"Make sure you phone me," she said. "I'm going to be moving back to Edinburgh, you know, and I want to see more of you." She kissed me once more and bit my lip playfully. And then she was gone.

I lay in bed for a long time staring at the ceiling and reliving the night before, step by step, with the aid of my own hands. The old woman from downstairs rang to complain about last night's banging. I let the answering machine take it. When I finally got up, I went to my computer and deleted the e-mail from Chris. I was more interested in the future now.

On the Care and Feeding of White Boys

R. Gay

It was an ordinary Thursday morning when my girlfriend and I decided that we wanted a white boy. She was drinking her coffee, and I was running from the bathroom to the bedroom and back trying to get ready. As I slipped a shirt over my head, Jasmine stuffed a piece of dry white toast into my mouth, kissed me on the cheek, and said, "We should try a white boy." I took a bite of my toast, swallowed hard, and wiped the crumbs from my lips. "That's not a bad idea," I finally said. So later that day, she called me at my office and suggested that we strategize as to how we were going to find the right white boy to bring to our bed. That night, she came home with a bag from Barnes & Noble. "Here," she said, handing me a book entitled *The Care and Feeding of White Boys: A Guide*. "They'll print anything," I said, but we sat on the couch anyway, and eagerly pored over the book's pages. Jasmine even took notes. Precision is very important to her.

White boys enjoy sporting events, particularly those where white and brown boys dressed in

tight-fitting pants shove each other across a large grassy field.

We decided to canvas the upcoming football game. It was homecoming weekend at the university; the stadium held 70,000 people, so logic dictated that we'd find at least 50,000 white boys of which we only needed 1. The numbers were on our side. But that weekend, as we froze under a cold and clear November sky, watching red-faced white boys with beer foam smeared across their lips and hoarse voices from cheering their team to victory, we realized that we needed a different approach. There was very little cream in the game-going crop.

Jasmine and I had discovered our mutual white boy fetish early on in our relationship. For our three-month anniversary I gave her a "Hollywood Hunks" videotape: four hours of tanned and greased white boys grinding and grunting toward ecstasy. I was nervous about the gift at first, but when she clapped her hands, immediately put the tape in the VCR, and proceeded to watch all four hours of the tape before dragging me to bed, I realized that I had indeed given a gift that would keep on giving. While we both acknowledged that we could never spend the rest of our lives with white boys, we concluded that there was something indescribably desirable about them—particularly ones who were lean and beautiful, relatively pale with enough hair to hold onto.

But we never acted on our forbidden fetish, mostly because we were afraid that the Lesbian Admissions Committee would rescind our toaster oven and membership cards. Instead, we titillated each other with loudly whispered fantasies of a white boy lying between our dark and softer bodies, as he slid his cock into our mouths, cunts, and asses and then left without asking to spend the night. We made a list of "Five Eligible but Unrealistic White Boys" we would bring home with us if all the world were a stage: Brad Pitt,

Keanu Reeves, Kevin Spacey, River Phoenix, and Edward Norton. And the book became invaluable.

> **White boys travel in packs, particularly when visiting large retail arenas known as shopping malls. They rely on each other for camaraderie and moral support in these retail arenas, particularly when in view of members of the opposite sex.**

Our second strategy was to patrol the two shopping malls in town. Unfortunately, our Saturday expedition proved fruitless. The white boys we found were too young, too attached, too dirty—so on and so forth. Our spirits were falling. What had seemed like a simple task was becoming quite an ordeal. The next week, Jasmine called and told me to meet her on campus for lunch. She held up the book, with a paragraph highlighted.

> **White boys are often ambitious because they carry with them a sense of entitlement. In an academic environment, they thrive in fields such as business, agriculture, and sports medicine.**

We decided to scope out the College of Business Administration. We met at the entrance armed with a Polaroid camera and legal pad. As I snapped pictures, she took notes. That night after dinner, we reviewed our selections. It was a tough choice. They all looked so clean-cut and eager, finely chiseled beneath T-shirts or polos and faded jeans. We finally decided on a tall, thin brunette feigning boredom as he ducked into his classroom. The picture we had was truly captivating. I was particularly enamored of the way his hair fell into his face and the wire-rimmed eyeglasses he wore, as if he was so far above his environs that he stayed out of mere spite.

We met at CBA for the next week, but were unable to find our chosen white boy. Again, our spirits fell, but I posited that perhaps our prey was a graduate student in a class that met once a week. The next Monday, we arrived early, and, as luck would have it, there he was, wearing corduroy slacks, a powder-blue dress shirt, those glasses, and a stunning expression of boredom. I wiped the palms of my hands against my jeans, squeezed my girlfriend nervously, and approached the white boy.

"Can I have a word?" I asked. He arched an eyebrow, and shrugged his shoulders. I nodded toward Jasmine. "We'd like to talk to you. We're recruiters," I said, lowering my voice. His expression of boredom lifted as he quickly agreed. We arranged to meet at a local bar for drinks later that night.

Jasmine and I were nervous, arriving at the bar half an hour early, easing our tension with gin and tonics, two ice-cubes, one lime. I held her hand under the table, idly tracing the thin lines of her palm as we at once hoped and dreaded that this was indeed the moment. He was fifteen minutes late, extending his hand in casual greeting. His first name was Mark. We didn't bother asking his last.

White boys are comfortable in the bar scene due to the overwhelming presence of fermented hops and members of their peer group. Statistics show that most white boys enjoy beer.

After he got himself a beer, the white boy sat across from us, crossing one leg over the other. "What company are you from?"

Jasmine and I exchanged a look. "We're not exactly from a company."

He leaned forward. "Are you headhunters?"

We nodded. "In a manner of speaking," I said. "We're in the process of recruiting one young man. There is no pay to speak of. But we would like to think that the benefits are enough."

Mark started to stand up. "I'm not interested in the Peace Corps."

I grabbed his wrist, feeling the bones lying just beneath his skin. "We're not with the Peace Corps."

He ran one hand through his hair and sat back down, taking a long sip of beer. "Can we cut to the chase? I have work to do."

I leaned back. "As do we."

Jasmine leaned forward. "To put it plainly, we're looking for a white boy, for one night. We picked you."

He arched both eyebrows into question marks. "For?"

I recalled the book's advice.

White boys prefer a direct approach. They lack a certain patience for the subtle nuances of flirtation.

"Again, to put it plainly, to fuck."

Mark coughed, spewing a stream of beer onto the table. "Come again?"

Jasmine stood up, circled the table and patted Mark on the back, gently massaging his shoulders, her lips hovering right next to his ears. "We want to fuck you."

He cleared his throat. "Why me?"

"Why not?" I asked.

Mark crossed his arms across his chest and shrugged his shoulders. His voice turned shy, "When do you want to do this thing?"

Jasmine and I smiled at each other. "Soon. Very soon."

"OK," he said weakly, his voice cracking.

Jasmine squeezed his shoulders harder. "We only have one question. Are you multiorgasmic?"

White boys are very sensitive about their sexual prowess, particularly in the face of cultural myths

about sexual organ size and performance. Exercise caution when broaching the subject of sexual performance.

Mark's face reddened from his hairline to his chin and he uncrossed his legs, nodding rapidly. "I can hold my own."

I handed him my business card, with our home number on the back. "Think about it, and give us a call. Saturday night works for us. We hope it works for you too."

Jasmine patted his shoulders one final time, and we left, leaving Mark at the table with his beer, bafflement, and a business card. We giggled like schoolgirls in the car. "I'm so hot," she whispered, sliding her tongue inside my ear as I tried to concentrate on the road.

"I am too," I murmured. Before I knew it, her hands were under the waistband of my pants and her fingers were on my clit as she told me all the nasty things we were going to do this weekend. We're lucky we made it home safely. She was very distracting.

Mark called two days later. We had almost given up on him and were making plans to attend the upcoming monster truck rally when the phone rang.

White boys are delighted when surrounded by noxious fumes and vehicles of exaggerated size. They are thereby afforded the opportunity to make loud noises and watch people do the things they wish they could do as well. (See *football*.)

"It's, uh, Mark," he said, quietly.

I smiled widely. "Mark! We were afraid we wouldn't hear from you."

"When do you want to do this?" he asked. "How does Saturday at seven sound?"

"I'll be there," Mark said, taking down our address.

When I got off the phone, I jumped into Jasmine's lap, kissing her face. "We don't have to go the monster truck rally! The white boy is coming."

"Well, I should hope so," Jasmine answered with a drawl.

"We're very bad girls," I whispered.

"There are worse things."

On Saturday, we were nervous. We tried to watch Lifetime movies to get a few extra pointers on white boys, but it was difficult to concentrate, with the prospect of our evening on our minds. Jasmine cleaned the house. I barbecued steaks and baked potatoes on the grill, then prepared a tray of fresh oysters and lemon.

> **Unless you have found a vegetarian, the white boy's meal of choice will include red meat and starches. If in doubt, sear the meat on the outside, leaving the inside a cool red. They feel that bloody meat enhances their masculinity and, while medical fact disproves such a belief, it does no real harm.**

Mark arrived fifteen minutes early, a fact we both noted with pleasure. While we ate, Mark and Jasmine engaged in a polysyllabic discourse on theories of effective group management. I stifled my boredom and studied our white boy. Mark had breathtaking, aquiline features. His eyes were a pale and watery blue that offset the light brown of his hair. His fingers were long and thin and looked incredibly soft, betraying the fact that he had probably never worked a hard day in his life. He wore a powder-blue dress shirt, again, plus khaki slacks and hiking boots, *the white boy uniform* in our part of the country, according to the book. When he spoke, his Adam's apple quivered, and I wondered what it would feel like beneath my lips.

As if she were reading my thoughts, Jasmine caught my attention and looked to the side. "Should we retire to the bedroom?"

Mark's eyes widened, and, I must confess, mine did too. Then I surprised myself. I became the kind of girl I always vowed I would never become. I unbuttoned the top two buttons of my shirt and leaned across the table, brushing my fingers across the top of Mark's hand. I raised my voice a few octaves, batted my eyelashes, and said, "Are you ready?"

"I've never done this sort of thing before," he said.

"Neither have we," Jasmine and I said, simultaneously. "That's part of the fun," she continued, standing up.

I took Mark's hand, and he quietly followed us into the bedroom. "That's a mighty big bed," he said as he took note of our king-sized bed.

"The better to fuck you on," I replied glibly.

I briefly wondered how horrified our parents and friends would be by this, which in turn turned me on.

"So do you want me to do one of you first, then the other?" he asked.

Jasmine clucked, shook her head, and put on some music. "Just follow our lead."

I stood in front of Mark, inhaled deeply, and slowly undressed, swaying my hips to the subtle rhythm coming from the stereo. Mark grinned shyly, then helped me slip out of my shirt, skirt, and panties as he did the white boy-overbite-dance. Jasmine stepped out of her clothes and lay on the edge of the bed, watching as I slowly unbuttoned Mark's shirt, kissing each new glimpse of pale, exposed skin. A thin line of hair ran from his navel to his waist, and I traced the trail with the tip of my tongue. He shivered, tentatively sliding his fingers through my hair. I pushed his hands away and stood, brushing my lips across his shoulders. He was tense, standing still as I pulled each of his nipples into my mouth, sucking them slowly and deliberately.

His breath caught in his throat, and I smiled, kissing the cleft of his chin before drawing my lips down his chest. It was odd, how different his body was from mine and Jasmine's. I was at once enraptured and repulsed by the smooth flatness of his chest, the quivering muscles of his torso, his tiny, pink, erect nipples. I sank to my knees, rubbing my face against the front of his slacks. It was as if I was trying to slow time. I unbuckled his belt, enjoying the sound of leather hissing against slacks. I carefully inched his zipper down, listening as the teeth of the zipper parted. I could feel Mark's cock against my cheek, not hard, but not soft, leaning against his left thigh.

He wore no underwear and I stared at his cock for a minute, moving to the side so that Jasmine's view remained uninterrupted. His cock was thick, perhaps seven inches in length, and light red. A soft down of blonde hairs covered his balls and crossed over to his inner thighs. I ran my fingers along his inner thighs, then started squeezing his balls, watching as the malleable flesh seeped through the spaces between my fingers. He groaned, loudly, and again took hold of my head, urging my mouth toward his cock. I licked my lips, smiled up at him, and kissed the tip of his cock before licking the small slit, tasting the silver sliver of pre-cum oozing from the tip. Mark's cock began to swell and, leaning forward, I wrapped my lips around the head of his cock and began suckling gently. He groaned again, tensing the muscles of his thighs, gripping my head more forcefully. Jasmine stood and moved behind Mark, pinching and twisting his nipples between her fingers as she grazed his neck with her teeth.

Mark bucked forward, and I carefully inched my mouth along his cock until my lips were pressed against his body. My throat muscles loosened around his girth and as the white boy began moving his hips, I bobbed my head up and down the length of his cock, tracing the thin veins with my tongue, squeezing his balls harder and harder.

"My God," Mark said, his voice strained. "I'm going to come."

"So soon?" Jasmine whispered, sliding her tongue along the sharp bumps of Mark's spine until she was also kneeling, brushing her lips across the small of his back.

"It feels too good," the white boy said, hoarsely.

I pinched the base of Mark's cock between two fingers, hard, and let his cock fall out of my mouth. "You can wait. Trust me, you want to wait."

His cock was rigid and throbbing and a violent red. His balls felt heavier in my other hand. I nodded toward the bed, and Jasmine climbed onto it, leaning into a pile of pillows against the headboard. I got on my hands and knees, shivering. I love the intimacy of such a vulnerable position. My forehead brushed against the tight curls of Jasmine's mound, and I nodded to Mark. "Take me from behind," I said softly.

White boys prefer a wide selection of condoms for the sexual act. It enables them to believe that they are sexually creative and adventurous.

On the nightstand sat the recommended wide selection: Trojans large and small, glow-in-the-dark condoms, condoms ribbed for her pleasure, condoms with innovative attachments dangling from the reservoir tip. He chose a ribbed condom, extra large, and tore the foil with his teeth, carefully sliding the latex onto his cock. For a moment, I was wistful, wishing we lived in a day and age where I could feel Mark's come shooting inside me and slowly oozing out as we both fell, exhausted, onto the sheets. I spread my thighs as far apart as I could, wantonly exposing myself, moaning as Jasmine caressed my forehead with her fingertips. I lowered my lips to hers, inhaling deeply. Mark knelt behind me and pressed his chest against my back, taking my breasts into his hands, massaging them, and rolling my nipples between his fingers. I felt a surge of wetness between my thighs and imagined myself flooding the bed—the three of us, found drowned in pussy juice, film at 11.

I reared toward Mark, silently urging him to enter me, and when he did, I gasped, feeling my cunt muscles stretching around his width. For some reason, I couldn't bring myself to look at Jasmine. Instead, I slid my tongue along the length of her pussy lips, from her clit to her ass, savoring the taste of her, gasping again as Mark pulled back and paused, the tip of his cock waiting at my entrance. My body quaked and I insistently rubbed my ass against Mark's hips. He slid one hand up my back, clasping the back of my neck, holding my hip with his other hand. He thrust forward again, harder and deeper this time. A dull ache began pulsing from somewhere inside my body, and I tried to move all the pleasure from my cunt to my mouth to Jasmine's cunt, swirling my tongue around her clit in furious circles.

He was a bit awkward at first, but Mark fell into a steady rhythm, putting his back into each stroke. As he tried to reach the deepest part of me with his cock, I tried to reach the deepest part of Jasmine with my tongue. Sweat fell from Mark's forehead to my back, slowly trickling into a small pool right above my ass. I tightened myself around him, and Mark took firm hold of my ass with both hands. He began thrusting so hard, I thought I might be shoved inside Jasmine's body. She raised her legs, resting her calves against my shoulders, her toes almost touching Mark's shoulders. Never in my life had I felt so surrounded by passion and flesh and fluid. Mark's thrusting grew more forceful. As his skin slapped against mine, I could feel him losing control. Jasmine's thigh muscles tightened and she wrapped her fingers through my hair, holding my mouth to her cunt as her hips bucked violently. I couldn't breathe. My tongue lacked a certain finesse, and as she came, she pushed me away and began trembling, cooing softly, as if she was exhaling for the first time that evening.

"I'm coming," Mark grunted, with one final thrust, holding himself inside me as his back arched. He fell onto my body and I fell against Jasmine. The three of us lay there, panting, sticking to each other, and silent. I danced along the unsatisfying edge of an orgasm, and I felt a twinge between my thighs so sharp, at once painful and sublime, that I was strangely glad that I hadn't come yet. Mark rolled off and lay on one side. I rolled to the other side, sliding my fingers into Jasmine's hand.

"That was incredible," Mark said.

"Indeed it was," Jasmine murmured. "But now I'm jealous. I want you inside me too."

Mark nodded slowly, wiping his forehead. "You've got to give me a minute."

I laughed, loudly, but my limbs felt heavy and wasted. "I suppose we can be patient."

I closed my eyes, resting my other hand across the soft swell of Jasmine's belly. Half an hour later, I felt Jasmine's lips brushing across my shoulder. I opened one eye, then the other, trying to gauge my surroundings. When I saw the sharp slope of the white boy's shoulder hovering above Jasmine's left side, I realized where I was, and smiled.

The white boy grinned proudly.

In sexual situations, white boys pride themselves when they are able to rejuvenate in a short space of time. Again, encouragement for their effort is highly recommended.

As if anticipating my next move, Jasmine placed her hand against Mark's breastbone and dragged her fingernails along his torso, across his waistline, and lightly over the soft heaviness of his cock. I watched as she wrapped her hand around his shaft and began stroking him slowly and steadily until he was again hard and throbbing. I handed her another condom and she tore open the foil, placing the condom between her lips before lowering her head to Mark's cock and sliding the condom along his length with her mouth.

"Neat trick," I whispered, and she smiled at me, arching an eyebrow.

"I know a lot of neat tricks."

I nodded my head to the side. "I don't doubt it."

Jasmine straddled Mark's lap, rocking her hips back and forth, letting her still wet pussy slide over his hips and groin. Leaning forward, she slid her hands up his chest, pushing his arms over his head. Then, holding Mark's cock between two fingers, she lowered herself onto him. I moved to my knees, kissing her sweaty arm, the shadowy side of her neck, her collarbone, then crawled up the bed and knelt over Mark's face, offering him a good look at the glistening, dark-pink tissues of my pussy. I could feel his ears against the sides of my knees, as I slowly sank into his mouth, moaning softly as I felt his tongue tentatively licking along my pussy lips. I looked up and saw Jasmine staring at me. Her face held an almost painful expression that insisted I stare right back at her. There was no smile on her face, only a look of passionate concentration that forced another spurt of wetness from my lips to Mark's.

Jasmine reached across the short distance between our bodies, taking my breasts into her hands and squeezing my nipples. I soon reached for her breasts. They felt heavy and full in my hands. I stared at her, almost in awe as I watched her seductively undulating along the shaft of the white boy's cock. The white boy became an object, and I wondered what we would look like to a voyeur—two dark women riding a pale, thin white boy, eyes only for each other. My entire body tingled as Mark groaned and began licking my clit, lightly at first, then harder and harder until I thought I would explode.

He paused, the painful pleasure subsiding until he began again. I began moving my hips apace with Jasmine, slowly, deliberately, with precision, punctuating each thrust by arching my back. It felt so sexy, knowing how hot we looked.

I could hear Mark moaning, groaning, and twitching beneath us. One of his hands was against Jasmine's left thigh; his other hand was against my left thigh. I felt myself about to come. I could tell that Jasmine knew exactly what I was feeling and that I knew exactly what *she* was feeling. We never broke eye contact. She was grinding against Mark and drifting toward me until our lips met. She tasted cool and sweet. At first it was as if we were sharing our first kiss, our tongues becoming entangled as we explored each other's mouths. We were kissing so hard that I knew the next day my lips would be bruised. I was trying to swallow her whole into my mouth, and she was trying to suck me into hers. As we came, we moaned into each other and—I swear—I felt her kissing the words *I love you* against my lips. As waves of pleasure rolled through my body, I slid forward, pressing my forehead against Jasmine's. My arms were wrapped around her neck, hers around my waist, and for what felt like hours we just sat there, atop the white boy, who slowly caught his breath, staring around the room, dazed and confused. He left shortly thereafter, thanking us profusely, asking if we could do it again sometime. We just smiled and closed the door after him.

**With proper care and feeding, white boys become
very loyal and obedient and take well to training.**

The Year of Fucking Badly
Susannah Indigo

"There is no such thing as bad sex," I say to no one in particular.

We're at the big oval table at the Empress Gardens, eating dim sum to celebrate the Chinese New Year when it all begins. It's the beginning of the Year of the Ox, a year that's supposed to bring the promise of new discoveries.

"Of *course* there is, Kenna," my friend Bill replies. "Bad sex: sex so awful, so unexpected, so terrible that just telling someone about it later makes them turn away in laughter, or horror."

"This really exists? Then why hasn't anyone ever made a whole magazine or something about it?" I can picture bad relationships, bad love, bad breakups, but not plain ol' bad sex, unless you're counting boring sex and then if you do, boring sex rules half the world and is the norm rather than the exception.

Bill pauses and puts his hand on my knee.

"You want me to show you, Kenna?"

I laugh. Bill is my sweet friend, my occasional fuck buddy, and about as obsessed with sex as I am. He's a Pig, as in the

Year of, defined quite appropriately as a sensual hedonist. I know this fact because I work as a research librarian—an "information specialist," they call us nowadays—and I get so many calls this time of year about Chinese astrology that I keep the chart by my desk.

I hike my black leather skirt a little higher as Bill watches, smiling.

"Hell, you know what I like, Bill. Most anything that moves." Even that is putting it mildly. "What exactly would you do to show me bad sex? Take me home and fuck me for five minutes in the missionary position and then roll over and say goodnight?" I don't talk this way around work, of course, where I wear my wavy red hair up in a bun, skip the leather, and leave the contacts home for my everyday glasses.

Bill offers to rape me if I want, which hurts my brain to think about. Everybody knows rape is not about sex. But if I let him rape me, is it still considered rape? I'm such a pervert I'd probably like it, no matter what.

"More stories!" says Bryan across the table from me, perhaps trying to deflect the conversation away from rape, which nobody ever talks about but most everyone fantasizes about.

"Define 'bad,' " Mary says. I wave my little librarian hand. At least I can add something to this.

"Did you know that the word *bad* is thought to originate from two Old English homophobic words from the thirteenth century—*baeddel* and *baedling*—which were derogatory terms for homosexuals, with overtones of sodomy?"

"Really?"

"Yeah." I can't recall why I remember this, but maybe, just maybe, it caught my attention because of the sodomy overtones.

Everyone at the table goes on to tell their own "bad sex" story. The boys' stories almost always involve not being able to get it up, but those strike me more as "bad imagination" or even "bad ego" rather than bad sex. Let's face it, women know. They sell enough cocks down at Good Vibrations to keep us girls happy for the rest of our lives.

I notice a trend. Every bad story seems to supply bare-bones details, elicits a gasp, and then trails off into "and it was so awful…."

I'm wracking my brain for a story of my own before my turn arrives. Nothing comes to mind, so I shrug and pass, and after a few more "it was awful"s the conversation turns to great sex. But the bad sex concept holds in my mind and I know there is no way to look this up at the library. Field research is required. I never pass on anything.

That's why people like me become researchers, because the urge to know everything and anything about a subject is overwhelming once it slips into that certain mind-curiosity-groove. If there's bad sex out there, I'll find it.

• • •

"It's sort of a scavenger hunt for bad sex, Holly," I try to explain to my upstairs neighbor and lover. We're buried deep under her pink comforter eating chocolate chip cookies the next night. Holly is the Martha Stewart of my love life—candlelight and cookies and flowers all the time.

Walking into her place is like walking into *Victoria* magazine. Some nights it's better than actual sex. She's a Dragon—as into mind-touching as she is into body-touching.

"Sometimes I have bad sex with myself," Holly offers. "You know, those nights when even your own fingers bore you to death?"

"Bad sex for one? Sounds like something Stouffers would make."

Monogamy is not a fetish of mine, but still I feel a little guilty even though Holly and I have always been open about any other lovers we might have. I decided a long time ago that two lovers was exactly the right number for me. My other lover is a student named Keith, a Snake like me but from a different generation, twelve years younger. He knows what I need. He likes to use my hair to tie me up in strange places before he fucks me, and I'm immensely fond of that particular knot.

Holly agrees it might be a good project as long as I promise only to attempt bad sex. She's an academic, so she decides to chart this all out for me. We decide that random bad sex would probably have to involve a stranger. We decide I need to keep a log of it all, and that there has to be a way to sort it out. She remembers the old Sears catalog ratings of "good/better/best" when buying products and decides that will do. Our final scale runs: Worst | Worse | Bad | Boring | Good | Better | Best—and that's it, I'm off for the hunt.

• • •

Driving down Broadway the first night, I sense one problem: I'm already wet at the promise of getting laid by someone new. I try to control myself by reciting the Dewey Decimal System out loud.

The lounge at the Holiday Inn on Colfax is the first stop. I'm wearing fishnet stockings and leather, but my hair is pulled back in a ponytail and my turtleneck rides high, a sort of combo slut/cheerleader look. It doesn't take me long to pick out a paunchy-looking, balding guy at a table by himself and start the flirtation.

He tells me his traveling salesman story, the exquisite details of selling hospital equipment, while I brush his leg with my boot and watch the surprise in his eyes at his luck. He's a Rat, I find out—outwardly cool, self-controlled but passionate.

"Push the button on my watch," he says, holding his wrist out for me to see.

I push the button.

"Tell me what it says, Kenna."

I'm stifling a laugh. Can I pick them or what? "It says, 'WANNA FUCK?'" And in capital letters, no less. "Pretty damn clever." I don't remember any mention of Rats having crass taste in jewelry.

"I had it made special in Taiwan."

Maybe, just maybe, I've found what I'm looking for, and on my first try. I don't want to sleep with him. So I will.

"Wow," I say, flipping my ponytail. "And, yes. But do you know where the word *fuck* comes from?" Now why on earth would I share this with him? But I do. "It's actually a mystery, but they think it might originally be from the Scandinavian *fokka*. There's one written record of the word in 1278, and then nothing—nothing at all until three hundred years later, maybe because it was such a taboo to say it." They probably didn't even make these watches back then.

He reaches over and twists my hair in his meaty hand and whispers, "I'll show you where fucking really comes from, sweetheart."

A kiss, the check, and he's guiding me to his room.

"Take off all of your clothes, lie down on your belly, and close your eyes," the Rat orders after we enter the tackiness that is room 413 at the Holiday Inn. "I want to show you something."

Another watch? His cock? Some strange hospital equipment? But this is my game, and I'm stripping down and stretching out.

He's searching in his bag and I'm peeking out of one eye and he's bringing out what looks like a bottle of oil.

"I used to work as a masseur," he says as he climbs up on top of me and begins with my back. "Let me massage this fine body, sweetheart." When his hands start in on me I see this boy starting to slide way up my sexual-rating chart. By the time he's worked me over with his oil, front and back, I'm completely limp in his hands and ready for anything and he's entering me from behind and riding me hard and holding my hair tight with one hand and slapping my ass with the other. He's got me hollering, "Fuck me, fuck me, fuck me," and I know that if this Rat had been around in the fourteenth century they would definitely have written the word down.

• • •

"OK, so looks aren't a good indicator of bad sex, Holly," I admit, safely back in her pink bed. "But what can I do—interview people and ask them if they're a lousy lay?"

Holly's reviewing my log. "All it says here is 'his hands, his hands,' Kenna."

"Shit, that's all I can remember. It was great."

She sighs, but we begin to plan the ex-lover possibility next. Julia was the love of my life ten years ago, until she decided she was too good for me and dumped me coldly. She's a Monkey—clever, witty, manipulative, and pretentious. The Chinese chart doesn't really say all that: I'm just projecting. I do distinctly recall her saying she was only going to sleep with Ph.D.'s after our breakup. And that she was only with me because she was crazy about my breasts. This has to be bad.

I find her at her modern dance class, where I show up in a low-cut black leotard to get her attention. I lie to her over lunch, tell her about my newly minted Ph.D. in the thirteenth-century dialect of Baedel Fokka, and get invited back to her place. I make up other stories for her about the places I've been and people I've met. When I create an imaginary friend-ship with Camille Paglia, whom I know she idolizes, I'm in. She spreads her legs for me and I'm devouring her and I sud-denly can't remember why I found her so attractive in the first place, but I go for the sex just to show her how hot I am, and it works.

When I leave and turn at the door to tell her, "I'm sorry, I won't be back, because I just realized that I should really only sleep with tenured professors," I realize that this is the most fun I've had in weeks.

• • •

I try to dive back into work and forget this whole idea, but every research question I'm asked sounds like sex. I've started watching everybody I see and thinking all the time about how they fuck, why they fuck, where they fuck, is it good, what do they do badly. When I'm not answering the phone I can be found doing some heavy breathing back in section 306.7, reading every sex book I can get my hands on. Hell, I'm so immersed in it I could practically write a thesis—maybe you *can* get a Ph.D. in Bad Sex.

• • •

Joe's Bait Shop is the local dive bar. Holly scoped the place for me over the weekend and thinks it's a guaranteed bad time. Every possible sport on a dozen big-screen TVs, pool tables in the back. The bartender's a babe. It's amazing how fuckable everyone looks when you're looking for people who aren't.

I'm wearing black tights, a long baby-blue sweater, black suede boots, and nothing underneath. I'm getting a few looks but no bites because of the damn football game. I forgot it was Monday night. Maybe this is bad sex, when you can't even draw a man away from the television.

I get myself a drink and wander toward the back room. There's some kind of a meeting in progress and no TVs, so I slip in and sit down in an empty card chair in the back to check out the crowd.

"My goal," the handsome man speaking says, "is to help others achieve sexual sobriety."

Wait, wait. Sexual *sobriety?* Is this where you only fuck before you get drunk?

"The twelve steps were my saving grace," he continues. "I turned my lust over to God."

Holy shit, I think I've wandered into a meeting of Overfuckers Anonymous.

I laugh. Heads turn in my direction, followed by frowns at my laughter. I can't help it. I know they're deadly serious. But maybe God knows what bad sex is. I wonder, does God like having all this lust turned over to him? Didn't God turn it over to us in the first place?

The speaker is looking right at me and smiling. "Who would like to share their story with us today?" He's got piercing green eyes and big shoulders and a fuzzy beard that I can already feel rubbing between my legs and I'm considering making up a quick, sad story to tell him and I know I should consider getting the hell out of here instead.

I do not volunteer. They'd never believe me if I told the truth about why I'm here. But, wait: bad sex, bad sex. These folks have potential. Oversexed people trying not to have sex could be really bad. Or would they be really good, heading toward Better/Best, like reformed Catholic girls let loose?

At the break, the speaker comes directly over to me and introduces himself.

"My name is Tony," he says with a gorgeous grin. Oh, my. I don't even have to ask, I know he's a Tiger, as in the Year of, the Hour of, the Moment of, the Bed of, the Cock of, and I'm heading for trouble.

"I just stopped in here accidentally," I say. "Giving up lust? This is like a bad dream."

"I know," the Tiger says. He pauses, asks my name, and then takes my arm firmly and guides me out toward the dark back corner of the bar where he chooses a stool. He smiles. "But I bet your dreams are spectacular, darling. You look like a girl who knows how to dream." Fresh drinks in hand, strong arms wrapped around me.

"Do you dream in color, Kenna?"

That's the best pickup line I've heard in ages. "Everyone does, Tony, or they can. Did you know that nobody ever questioned this fact before the advent of black-and-white television in the fifties? Not Freud, not Jung...." I hear my little librarian voice being smart, yet at the same time I feel my knees shaking like a little girl and I just want to climb up on his lap and let him turn his lust over to me instead of God.

He listens to me as though every word I utter is golden. He knows the secrets: words and hands and eyes and laughter. Attention paid; intensity gained. But it keeps sneaking through the haze of my desire that this man is one of them.

"Tony, didn't I just hear you discussing 'sexual sobriety' as a way of life?" I ask as he pulls me onto his lap. His hand goes higher and higher on my thigh. It's so high and so right that I think I imagined it all, and that this is my punishment, or maybe my reward, for thinking and dreaming about sex day and night and pretending I know a single thing about what it all means.

"For you, darling, I'm willing to fall off the chastity wagon." His mouth is on mine and he's biting my lip with the force that I need and I am going, going, gone. I don't believe a word he says and I don't care. The cock of the Tiger is hard beneath my ass and all the lines are slipping away and Good is blending into Better and heading off the chart and he's whispering in my ear and I want it all. Finally we're out the door.

Before he starts the car he says, "Pull your tights down and spread your legs and let me see." I do and he just watches me. When he stops the car at Sunset Park a short drive away and leans over, his beard is rough against my thighs—exactly as I imagined it—and he's biting and sucking and I'm in heaven and then he's suddenly slowing way down.

"I shouldn't do this," he mumbles with his mouth still buried in my pussy. Oh, God, I think—maybe this is the bad sex I deserve, when it begins to orbit off the chart and you know that somehow when it's over it's going to wrap right back around and come up on the awful horrifying side as chastity reclaimed.

"I shouldn't do this," he repeats, and I think maybe he's waiting for me to save him. This is one of those damned defining moments in life. Define the moment or it defines you. Screw him, or screw him? Fuck it. Or fuck me.

I reach down and stroke his hard cock through his jeans.

"I'll be good for you, Tiger. Don't stop, don't stop." He lifts my sweater and we're tumbling toward the back seat like teenagers in lust and I'm not sure I'll be able to excuse this behavior later as research but maybe I don't even care. My tights are off and my legs are wrapped high around his big shoulders and his cock presses into me. He leans down and begins to bite my nipple and to send me over the edge. He pauses and I think I will die if he stops one more time.

"You're right, darling," he whispers, driving into me hard. "For tonight, there's no such thing as bad sex."

About the Authors

LISA ARCHER's work appears in *Best Women's Erotica 2002* and numerous other publications, including *Bad Subjects, Black Sheets, GettingIt.Com, HIV InSite, NOW Toronto,* the *San Francisco Bay Guardian, ScarletLetters.com,* and *VenusOrVixen.com.* Lisa Archer is a pseudonym.

JEN COLLINS writes short erotic fiction (a.k.a. smut) and creative nonfiction essays, and maintains a love–hate relationship with poetry. Her work has appeared in *Set in Stone: Butch-on-Butch Erotica* and *Young Wives' Tales: New Adventures in Love and Partnership*, as well as a handful of periodicals. She lives in southern Maine with her partner, Anna.

SUSAN COSS is a San Francisco writer and a returning reader at the annual Pussy Lips Breast Cancer Benefit. This is her first published story.

NINE DECLARE was born in Northern Ireland in 1977 and graduated in sociology with gender studies from the University of Edinburgh. Sadly, she is better known for her hair than for her writing. She can be found at www.awkwardsilence.org.uk.

ERICA DUMAS has written erotica for *Sweet Life: Erotic Fantasies for Couples* and the forthcoming *Noirotica 4*. In addition to writing, she plays several musical instruments and listens to lots and lots of jazz.

ASTRID FOX lives in London. She is the author of the novels *Rika's Jewel, Primal Skin,* and *Cheap Trick*. She has also had erotic short stories published in *Sugar and Spice 2, Wicked Words, Viscera, The Mammoth Book of Lesbian Erotica,* and *Wicked Words 4*. The polymorphously perverse thirty-two-year-old once clocked in a personal celibate best of two and a half years, although these days she leads a wicked, sinful life.

R. GAY is a writer and editor living in the Midwest. Her work can be found—past, present, or forthcoming—in *Clean Sheets, Scarlet Letters,* and the anthologies *Herotica 7, Does Your Mama Know?, Sweet Life: Erotic Fantasies for Couples, Best Transgender Erotica,* and others. She unabashedly admits to having a fetish for white boys.

ESTHER HAAS is a slut-about-town and low-stakes black-jack player who, when not dreaming of hitting the progressive jackpot on a Betty Boop quarter slot, likes to dabble in porn. This is her first published story.

ARIEL HART was born and ill-bred in Brooklyn, New York, where she lives with her husband and son. Her works of fiction, nonfiction, and poetry have appeared in publications like *Seventeen* and *Screw*—and practically everything else in between. She has also written close to one hundred produced adult screenplays.

THEA HILLMAN's writing has appeared in *Berkeley Fiction Review, On Our Backs*, and the *San Francisco Bay Guardian*. She has performed her work at poetry slams, bookstores, literary festivals, and other venues throughout the United States. She has also performed a birdcall on the *Tonight Show with Jay Leno;* has appeared on the cover of the Oakland, California, phone book; and holds a tag-team haiku championship title.

SUSANNAH INDIGO is editor-in-chief of *Clean Sheets Magazine* (www.cleansheets.com) as well as the editor of the *Slow Trains* literary journal (www.slowtrains.com). Her writing has appeared in many anthologies, including *The Best American Erotica, Herotica*, and *Best Women's Erotica*. She is also a contributor to *Salon Magazine*. See her website for more information: www.susannahindigo.com.

MARILYN JAYE LEWIS's novellas and short stories have been widely anthologized in both the United States and the U.K. *Editions Blanche* (Paris) will publish the French language edition of her critically acclaimed collection of novellas, *Neptune and Surf*, in fall 2001. She is coeditor of *The Mammoth Book of Erotic Photography* and is the winner of Best Erotic Writer of the Year in the U.K. As webmistress, her erotic multimedia sites have won numerous awards. Visit her website: www.marilynjayelewis.com.

LYNN A. POWERS holds a master's degree in art history from Virginia Commonwealth University and has not accomplished much with it except to write her first published nonfiction book, *Killer Art: Art That Has Maimed, Killed, and Caused General Destruction Throughout the Centuries.* She is at work on two novels and resides in New Orleans with her husband, David, and their two dogs, Newman and Whisker Puss.

CAROL QUEEN got a doctorate in sexology so that she could impart more realistic detail to her smut. She is the author of many erotic stories, as well as essays and sex information. For a complete listing, check www.carolqueen.com. When not writing, she works at Good Vibrations, and she and her partner, Robert, are working on founding a new organization called the Center for Sex and Culture.

RACHEL RESNICK is the author of the *Los Angeles Times* listed best-selling novel *Go West Young F*cked-Up Chick* (St. Martin's) and is a contributing editor at *Tin House Magazine.* She's had fiction, plays, and nonfiction published in the *Los Angeles Times, Tin House, The Ohio Review, Chelsea, Absolute Disaster: Fiction from LA,* and *LA Shorts,* among others. "Scenes from Thailand" is an excerpt from her new novel-in-progress, currently titled *Education of a Cunt.* She lives in Topanga Canyon, up the street from where Charles Manson used to park his bus. Visit her website: www.rachelresnick.com.

MICHELLE SCALISE has sold nearly two hundred poems and short stories to magazines and anthologies such as *The Darker Side; Viscera; Bell, Book, and Beyond; Darkness Rising;* and *Best Women's Erotica 2001.*

HELENA SETTIMANA lives in "The Big Smoke," Toronto, Ontario, with her partner of many years and a tiger tribe of four. When not writing erotica, or teaching, she poses as a potter, painter, and clay sculptor. Her website is located at http://evilzz.net/hsettimana.

ELISE TANNER's poetry has appeared in *Sensibilities, West Coast Review, The North Coast Literary Review*, and *Illusions*. She has also written erotica under various names for *Taboo Letters* and other publications. She lives on the north coast of California with her lover.

LANA GAIL TAYLOR lives in Colorado with a lazy cat, an adorable son, and a whole lot of Poison, Slaughter, and Ratt CDs. Her erotic short stories have appeared in *Playgirl Magazine, Dare for Women, Cleansheets.com, Mind Caviar.com* and *Bedroom Eyes: Lesbians in the Boudoir*. Meanwhile, Lana is writing as much as possible and insists she isn't wearing any spandex.

JOY VANNUYS is the pseudonym of a chef and food writer who lives in Brooklyn, New York.

About the Editor

CARA BRUCE runs Venus Or Vixen Press and the erotic web magazine *VenusOrVixen.com*, which won the *San Francisco Bay Guardian*'s Best of the Bay 2000 prize. She is the editor of *Viscera* and publisher of *Embraces: Dark Erotica*. She is coauthor, with Lisa Montanarelli, of *The First Year: Hepatitis C* (Morse & Co.). Her fiction has appeared in numerous anthologies, including *Best American Erotica 2001; Best Women's Erotica 2000, 2001, and 2002; Best Lesbian Erotica 2000; The Unmade Bed: Twentieth Century Erotica; Starf*ckers; Uniform Sex; The Oy of Sex; Best S/M Erotica; Mammoth Best of the Year Erotica; Hot and Bothered 3;* and *Noirotica 4.* Her nonfiction has appeared in *Salon.com,* the *San Francisco Bay Guardian, While You Were Sleeping, On Our Backs,* and *Bust,* among others. She is the editor of *Good Vibrations Magazine.* She is also editing *Obsessed: Fetish Erotica* for Cleis Press. She is very busy but always makes time for the best bisexual sex.